The Town that Never was...

by Lee M. Cooper

This is a work of fiction. Names, characters, businesses, places, events, and incidents are either the products of the author's imagination or used in a fictitious manner. Any resemblance to actual persons, living or dead, or actual events is purely coincidental.

All rights reserved. No part of this book may be reproduced or used in any manner without the prior written permission of the copyright owner, except for the use of brief quotations in a book review.

Copyright © 2024 by Lee M. Cooper

BY LEE M. COOPER

Contents

Monday February 5th 2

Wednesday February 7th 10

Thursday February 8th 17

Friday February 9th 26

Monday February 12th 32

Thursday February 15th 40

Wednesday March 6th 46

Monday April 8th 53

Tuesday April 9th 61

Wednesday April 10th 68

Thursday April 11th 77

Friday April 12th 80

Saturday April 13th 91

Sunday April 14th (AM) 105

Sunday April 14th (PM) 112

Date Unknown... 128

The Day I Escaped... 136

Tuesday August 20th 143

BY LEE M. COOPER

Monday February 5th

Sitting at my desk, I stared into my hot cup of freshly made coffee. One good thing about coffee at the office, is that it wasn't that cheap, nasty crap either. It's actually pretty good, it's about the only good thing being here. Listen to me, this is so stupid. It's like I'm trying too hard to take my mind off of what's happened, but the shrink insisted that this is the best starting point on the road to recovery. So, since we are starting at the beginning of this diary, and to whomsoever gives a crap about reading this in the future, I'll fill you in on what's happened, shall I?

My name is Christian Hawk, and seven days ago I lost everything that meant anything to me. My fiancé Rachael, died in a car accident. Some lowlife, middle-aged drunken scumbag drove straight into the side of her at a junction. The car was hit with such force, that it flipped down the side of a hill, with close to eleven rotations, so they

BY LEE M. COOPER

said. She died later that night... I managed to get to the hospital before she went. I felt the warmth that she always carried with her leave in an instant. And when that warmth left, a piece of me left with her too that night. If they ever catch the murderer who did this, they better hope it's not whilst I'm on duty...

The past few days have mainly been taken up with funeral arrangements, speaking to our friends and breaking the tragic news. I constantly find myself stopping, be it in the street, around the house, today at work. It just hits me like a hammer every now and again, but I know I have to carry on. I have to be strong for the loved ones still around me. I have to keep up strength at work as a police officer, and continue on as best I can, to do my duty. I've been seeing a head doctor now on and off for the past three or so years. It was something that the force encouraged us to do as officers, to help deal with the trauma we sometimes have to cope with in our work. Though, this past week, I think I saw Dr Nielson more than I have in the past five months!

Yesterday was the funeral. It was simple yet beautiful, just how she wanted it in her will. It was quickly organised and kept quite small. It was also perhaps the hardest day of my life so far. I still can't understand that my wife to be, was being lowered into the ground. All the upset family, our

BY LEE M. COOPER

closest friends, her parents...it just seems so surreal to me. As though it was some kind of scene from a TV show or something. I said my farewells to her in private, and I know that she will always be with me in my heart and watching over me.

    Listen, to whoever reads this, I don't want to dwell on the bad times. I'm sure as I go on, I may even reminisce on more of the good times. They will be what will stay with me for as long as I live on. So here I am back in the station office today, everybody has been about the usual amount of supportive as you would expect. Lots of flowers and cards, but I have come back in as soon as I have, to try and take my mind off of things. And the best way I've always done that in the past, was to throw myself into my work and try and help somebody else out. Perhaps I can stop the next poor soul from being the victim of a hit and run, hell, maybe I can even catch the bastard responsible for...no, no I need to try and stay focused for now.

    Around ten-thirty, my captain came out to see me. Captain Patrick Mulherny. A nice guy really, a little old school and firm but fair and very by the book.

    "Christian, how you doing? I know that's a silly question, but I just wanted you to know that we are all

BY LEE M. COOPER

obviously thinking about you and if you need anything, anything at all you just let me know, ok?"

He definitely sounded concerned, usually you can cut right through the bullshit with him, but he was actually being sincere.

"I'm ok thanks captain, just ploughing my head into work is the best cure I can get right now, thanks," I tell him.

"Sure! Sure! Well, hey, I just had a thought. Step inside my office would you Hawk?"

Hmm, "this can't be a good thing" I thought to myself, as I stood and walked across the room into his office. His blinds were always down so you could never tell what he was saying when he asked anybody in. I straightened my tie and strolled on in, as I closed the door behind me.

"Listen. Something came across my desk this morning. A new case, it's quite an unusual one but I've been thinking of who to assign it to. Maybe a trip outta town might do you good, son?"

BY LEE M. COOPER

A 'trip outta town' he said. Well maybe this could be just the thing I need to get away from everything right now. I sat down and pulled in my chair as he continued.

"I'm all ears sir."

"Good, good. It's a missing persons case, apparently, it's gone through several stations with no one taking any great interest in it. You see, the strange thing is that when I tell you it's out of town, I actually mean it's in a small town called Holberg, just north of mainland Norway."

"Norway! Sir? But we are just a normal precinct in Chicago? Why would a case like this come to us, or anyone in the states for that matter?"

"Well, that is a good question Hawk. The truth is there are only so many people that a) would want to take on this particular case and b) are even qualified for it."

"But sir, what do you mean exactly?"

He gave me a strange smile and looked down at his desk while he chuffed on a cigar, as though he knew more than he was willing to let on to me.

BY LEE M. COOPER

"Well, you see Christian, you're a talented individual, who is one of the few that have undertaken the governments new rigorous 'Alpha Rescue Tactics' programme, or 'ART' as they call it for short. Now as I understand it, you came out of that with top grades and fast-tracked straight here to us around five years ago now. Every now and again, these kinds of cases are opened up internationally to see if anyone wants to take them on. Not many people have your sorts of skills, but to me, they sound just the ticket for this!"

That was an awful lot of information to digest in my already clouded head, but the opportunity to get away still seemed to resonate with me, so I pressed him for more information.

"That's right captain, they taught us many skills in the field and specialised particularly in negotiation, rescue, close quarters combat and even various medical techniques. It was a good programme sir for sure, and one I'm very grateful I was a part of. What else can you tell me of the case exactly?"

"Well, seventeen people have gone missing in this Holberg town in the last few months. None of their local police can seem to find them anywhere and a whole host of strange signs were left behind by each disappearance. It doesn't go into too much detail in the paperwork, but the higher ups have asked if we want to send anybody over there to investigate. Listen, its entirely up to you and I know it's a little quiet around here lately but if you're interested, then there's nobody on the force I can think of who would be better suited to this. However, by the same token, if you aren't interested then…"

I stopped him instantly. I don't know why, just something inside me told me to stop him right away and take it on.

"No, no that's fine sir. I've heard all I need to; I'll take it on if that's ok with you sir?"

It seemed to cheer him up more than me, as he showed a wide-eyed grin and smacked his hand on the desk in what seemed like delight. Then again, he was always the competitive type…probably happy if someone from his office could solve this and give him something to gloat about over the other precincts in the area.

"Aha! Splendid son, just splendid. Here's the papers for you to run over but if you want to get some provisions packed, you can leave as soon as you're ready."

BY LEE M. COOPER

"Thank you, sir. Give me a day and I'll be on the next flight out," I tell him. After all, I have nothing to hang around for and the mental distance from home will do me good.

BY LEE M. COOPER

Wednesday February 7th

After a couple of days travel and a few delays on my flight, it hadn't taken me long to get packed up and arrive at Holberg. It seemed strange that I didn't have to tell Rach that I'd be away on work or make any other arrangements at such short notice. My world now, seemed so much smaller all of a sudden.

After an hour or so taxi ride from the airport and then a further two-hour boat ride from the mainland across to the island of 'Smola' and then ANOTHER taxi ride, I finally arrived at the town of Holberg. And my god was it cold, -15 degrees, the taxi said. As the driver pulled up just on the outskirts of the town, he rather abruptly got out and opened the door for me and then proceeded to get back in his seat and popped the trunk open for me. Thanks, I suppose that's about as warm of a welcome as I'm going to get here. After I got my case out of the trunk, the driver didn't hang around, the man went screeching off down the road swerving left and right in the ice. What was his deal? I remember thinking

BY LEE M. COOPER

he'd perhaps played crazy taxi too much in his younger years or something.

As I looked around, there was a thick fog that seemed to be apparent around the whole area, and I stood at what appeared to be the foot of some concrete steps, leading up to the town's main gates. It was so quiet; you could almost hear a pin drop. It was early evening now and I decided that my best approach would be to source out my hotel for the evening, get unpacked, take a hot shower, eat a good meal and then find the local police station in the morning. As I approached the towns opened gates, I couldn't help but notice they appeared to have intricate engravings on them. One gate showed what appeared to be Mjolnir, the mighty hammer of the Norse thunder god Thor. On the other gate, an emblem with which I was more unfamiliar with. It looked like an open wolfs mouth of some sort, baring teeth, although, I could be mistaken. Whatever it was, it didn't look very inviting.

As I made my way onto the main street, looking around the thick fog, I could only make out vague building shapes and nothing obvious that seemed like street signs or directions of any kind. I decided to carry on forwards and follow my way down what looked to be the main street. The day was still light, so no streetlamps were lit to speak of, but

BY LEE M. COOPER

towards what seemed to be the market square, the fog dissipated a little. This town looked very historical, very old looking buildings, and now what appeared to be a few actual life forms about. Making my way towards an elderly gentleman, who was sat on a bench alone, I decided to ask him for directions to the hotel.

"Excuse me sir, do you speak English?" I asked the well-dressed, grey-haired man.

He wore a fedora hat, and a white, smart dressed shirt underneath a waistcoat and tweed jacket, with trousers to match. Must've been around his mid-eighties if I had to guess. I'm not sure if he didn't hear me, so I continued again to ask the gentlemen.

"Sorry, sir? My name is Christian, I'm looking for the 'Pearl hotel'? Do you know where that is please?" I loudly spoke to him.

The old man simply continued to stare into the fog for a moment, and then slowly turned his head to me and smiled. Then he pointed behind me, he was quite creepy if I'm being honest. Turning around to look over my shoulder, I then saw a board flapping over the doorway of a distinguished looking building, with the aforementioned pearl picture upon it.

BY LEE M. COOPER

"Thank you, sir!" I shouted back at him.

But he simply returned back to his posture of looking directly ahead into thin air. With nothing further to say in our somewhat 'lengthy' discussion, I decided to cut the meeting short and head straight to the hotel.

Upon pushing open the wooden door, and stepping into a bar area, things didn't get any less weird. There was a musty smell in the place, wooden beams ran along the ceiling and a few old drinking tankards hung from above the bar. It certainly seemed a quaint kind of place, the floor was carpeted from what looked like the seventies and the handful of people present all stopped drinking and looked at me. As I smiled and nodded to the local patrons, I may as well have been acknowledging a bunch of ghosts, for all the return I got back.

Deciding to try to get some sense from the bartender, I turned and walked to the bar.

"Hello, my name is Christian..."

"Yes, Mr Hawk of course. We have been expecting you here."

BY LEE M. COOPER

The man's interjection took me by surprise, especially as his English was so perfect sounding. I couldn't even pick up much of an accent. His bright, welcoming smile was a stark contrast from the zombie like locals I'd encountered so far. The guy seemed well informed of my arrival in any case and appeared quite formal in a suit and tie, dark slicked back hair and clean shaven.

"Oh, thank you. Yes, that's me," I replied with a smile of relief that someone at least was expecting me.

"Very good sir, we do not get many visitors here. I do apologise for the vague looks you may get. You must seem very strange here, especially all the way from America!"

I chuckled nervously at him with a smile. Already this seems a very strange place. Nothing like anywhere I've seen in the states before, that's for sure.

"If you will follow me sir, your room is ready upstairs."

Thanking him for his kindness, I followed him up to my room. The stairs creaked and the banister at the top was quite wobbly. He opened the door for me and gestured a welcoming hand to go on inside. At first glance, the room was

BY LEE M. COOPER

fairly small and simple. A single, yet rather inviting looking bed. Warm looking curtains, a view overlooking the market square, an en-suite, and some cupboards for storage. Oh, and a TV, though I'm not sure what kind of channels I'll pick up out here, if any!

"Please, make yourself comfortable sir. I do hope you find everything you require, however please do let me know should you require anything further Mr Hawk."

"Thanks..." I stumbled.

"Oh, I do apologise, where are my manners. My name is Fredrik, by the way."

"Ah, thank you Fredrik. There is one question I do have, relating to my work. Where is the local police station here?" I asked him.

The man paused for a second with a brief look of pain on his face, before he straightened himself out and replied with a smile once again.

"The police station sir, you are a police officer?"

BY LEE M. COOPER

"I am. I'm here on important business regarding some missing persons reports. Do you know about them?"

"I see sir, yes, we did hear of the missing people of whom you speak. Terrible business, all of that. Sons & daughters, mothers & fathers all going missing. The police station is just to the right of the market, follow the road up and you will come upon it on the right shortly thereafter. Hopefully, the fog should clear by the morning, sir."

I nodded and thanked him once again for his help, but then he said something pretty strange to me, as he turned to leave the room.

"I do hope you manage to find the answers you seek and bring justice to our town. I must warn you though, this town has a very long history and many strange stories about it. Please do be careful what answers you unearth. Sleep well sir."

Well, if that wasn't food for thought, I don't know what was. I figured that I'd find my own answers soon enough, starting in the morning. Superstitions don't frighten me. Just cold, hard killers are what I lose sleep over at night.

BY LEE M. COOPER

Thursday February 8th

The nightmares occur now, every night since it happened. I woke up this morning after a broken night's sleep, in a cold sweat. The bed was comfortable enough, but it just isn't the same sleeping alone. Must've been around 4am, I decided to just get up, grab a coffee and prepare for a busy day ahead. Looking out my room window, it was still pretty dark outside but as Fredrik said yesterday…it does look like the fog's cleared a bit now. I saw the bench that I spoke to the old man on yesterday, it looked like the same man was still sat there. Even had the same clothes on, had he really been there all night?

I decided to skip breakfast and grab something whilst I was out, I was intrigued to find the town's station and get to work. After I got changed and prepared my belongings for the day, I scampered down the stairs and bumped into Fredrik by the front desk on my way out. He asked if everything was satisfactory, to which I simply told him.

"Just fine, thanks."

BY LEE M. COOPER

He bowed his head slightly and gave me a slim smile. Something about that guy gives me the creeps, I just don't know what yet. I stepped outside and breathed in the cool, fresh air. Oddly enough, the elderly gentlemen on the bench had now disappeared and the square appeared empty, now dimly lit by a few lamp posts. As sure as Fredrik said yesterday, I soon found the towns police station, right where he said it would be. From the outside, the building looked, in keeping with the rest of the town, very old. It seemed well kept enough, save for a few broken slabs on the floor outside and a slightly crooked wall. Nevertheless, I decided to press on and opened a small waist high gate and proceeded to ring the doorbell. There were lights on from what I could see through the two front windows, so I definitely knew there was at least somebody in. I waited a couple of minutes before ringing again, however upon the second ring, the door swung open mere moments afterwards. An oddly pasty-faced guy stood there, smartly dressed enough in his full police uniform but a rather vacant look upon his face. I decided to break the awkward silence as quickly as I could.

"Hi, excuse me I wasn't sure if anyone heard my first ring, ha. My name is Christian Hawk, I believe I'm expected? I'm from the Chicago grand central police force."

BY LEE M. COOPER

"Ah yes, of course. Apologies, I'm constable Andersen. Come on in, I'll let the chief know you're here. I do hope your trip wasn't too much trouble, we are quite out in the middle of nowhere here."

He showed me in, and I followed him down a narrow corridor which had branching offices off from it. The station seemed relatively small but ample for the size of the town, I guess. The chief's office was labelled at the end of the hallway, 'Chief Larsen' the door said. Andersen knocked a couple of times and then a shout came from inside.

"Come on in."

He opened the door for me and parted with a nod, as I walked into the Chiefs office. I was greeted by a somewhat large man, looked around his mid-fifties with a short dark beard and hair, with whips of grey in both. Again, the chief also appeared well dressed and was stood by his window next to his desk.

"Ah, Mr Hawk I believe. Please come on in and take a seat," he said, in a down-to-business sort of way yet friendly enough all the same.

"Thank you" I replied.

BY LEE M. COOPER

"Tell me Mr Hawk, how was your journey? I do hope it was a pleasant one. You must be quite tired after your long journey?"

"Oh, it was fine," I lied. I was tired and the journey was pretty uncomfortable to say the least, yet I was eager to crack on with the case.

"Good, good. Well, we appreciate you coming all the way here, so I'll get right down to business. I have on my station's hands, seventeen missing people. These people range in age from twenty years old through to seventy-six years old. They have each disappeared over the course of three months, at various different locations. There are no visible connections between any of them and at their last known locations, we have seen very odd traces left behind."

He was deadly serious as he explained all of this to me, and I found myself even more intrigued.

"Odd traces, chief Larsen? Please can you elaborate on what you mean by odd?"

The man sighed as I asked this, as though the mere thought was a great toll on him.

BY LEE M. COOPER

"I think it perhaps best if I show you..."

Later in the afternoon, the chief took me to one of the earlier scenes, of the last known location of a Ms. Ingrid Hagen. The chief drove us to her apartment, it was quite a newly built apartment block, very clean looking from the outside. After we made our way up to the fourth floor, we were greeted by some police tape across the doorway and an officer on guard duty.

After allowing us in, I took a look around the entrance area which led into a newly furbished kitchen. I looked at the chief with a slight confused look, as I gazed around, I couldn't see anything out of place. If anything, the apartment seemed completely spotless.

"Chief, what exactly is wrong with this place? It all seems pretty normal to me so far from what I can see?"

He pursed his lips together inwards.

"You better look in here, officer Hawk."

He then opened a plain white door just off the apartment's hallway, into the bathroom...as I looked on in utter shock. The bathtub had completely split with what looked like, three giant claw marks cutting straight through it. The marks also continued to appear on the walls, as though some sort of animal had torn the room apart.

"S...sir, what could have done this? A wild...bear of some sort?"

"That's just the thing, there's no native animal of any kind anywhere near Holberg, that has a claw pattern to match this size or trajectory. And the fact that it's only in this room is also quite baffling, wouldn't you agree?"

I have to admit, I'd never seen anything like this in all my years of service. The window was open but there was no sign of blood or any other foul play.

"Have you taken any forensics of any kind chief?"

"Yes, we scoured the whole area. The marks included. And that's the other weird thing, the forensics couldn't bring up anything. No hair, no skin, no fluids of any kind. Nothing."

My face scrunched in absolute confusion. This was going to take some figuring out, no doubt about it. Though my first thought in working out the next step, was to ask about the other sites to see if there would be any connections that could possibly be made.

"Chief Larsen, could you give me the list of addresses for all of these missing persons? I'd like to carry out my own personal investigations, and I don't want to keep taking up all of your time naturally."

"Of course, officer Hawk," he said.

"However, after all our findings, I shall highlight the ones that have differentiating circumstances. Not all of these places have the same traces of what you have found here, and likewise a few do. I feel it may help speed up your investigations, wouldn't you say?"

"That's very kind of you chief Larsen," I replied.

"Excellent, then I shall have the list written up this afternoon, that way you can proceed first thing in the morning however you so wish. For now, I'll wait in the car and let you peruse around here a little longer, yes?"

I nodded and gave him a brief smile, to which he then left me alone in the room. I looked out the window, the view was a pleasant one overlooking the towns fishing bay. A few

BY LEE M. COOPER

boats floated idly at the dock and a few fishermen were sat patiently waiting for a catch. Hmmm, there's no real reason anyone would try to enter from the window, it doesn't look very accessible and seems far too public, in view of the dock area. I felt the grooves of the three cuts. They measured roughly three inches wide, the length was hard to tell, though looking at the wall markings they must've been at least three feet long! They didn't feel smooth like a blade of any kind, as the inner slash markings had a very fine serration to them. Nevertheless, whatever made these markings, certainly didn't appear to struggle as they cleaved right through a solid stone bathtub.

Later that evening, after spending a few more hours looking over the apartment, I decided to return to my room at the hotel and write up my findings. The chief was kind enough to drop me back off at the 'Pearl hotel,' and we made arrangements to reconvene first thing in the morning to run through the list of addresses. As I got out the car and it pulled away, I once again saw the old man sat on his bench, staring aimlessly into the air. I remember thinking he must really, really like that bench!

I snuck past Fredrik as he was attending to the bar, I wasn't in the mood for idle chit chat and just wanted to get pen to paper, as it were. 8pm came around and I'd had dinner

BY LEE M. COOPER

brought to my room that evening, it was a very nice, seasoned chicken with vegetables and potato fritters. After a hot shower and having written down my notes, I turned to put my personal thoughts down into this diary. The work today has helped take my mind off of things a little bit, but I still feel the sense of loneliness overcome me late at night and at moments like now. If I were working away, I'd perhaps pick up the phone and call Rachael, to see how her day went. I guess it's just a part of me that will have to find a way in time, to deal with it.

BY LEE M. COOPER

Friday February 9th

My alarm clock rang this morning at 6am. Though I needn't have used it, for all the sleep I actually got. The nightmares I am having when I do sleep, are getting more vivid. I see her, Rachael, lying there in a burning car screaming for me to help her...but every time I get there too late, and the car explodes. I don't know if this is pure guilt, or if there's any kind of meaning behind all this. Dr Nielson, my shrink, would probably say there's a connection of some kind, though what exactly that is, I do not know at present.

As I got out of bed and opened the curtains, I was greeted by a wet start to the day. Rain was lashing it down outside in the market square, but by my sheer amazement, the creepy old guy was still sat on the bench! I feel like I need to ask Fredrik about him if I see him today. It makes me wonder, with all the time he spends sitting there in all weathers, if he's actually seen anything strange in the last few months. That's if I can actually find a clairvoyant around here to actually communicate with the old timer.

After a quick shave and getting dressed, I made my way downstairs to breakfast. The hotel had rearranged a small room off from the bar area for a buffet style breakfast. I was the only one in there so of course, Fredrik was once again on standby, just for me. He almost felt like my PA at times on this venture so far.

"Good morning, Mr. Hawk, how goes your investigations?" he asked, whilst bringing me over a hot cup of coffee.

"Well, it's early days but I have a few leads I need to chase up today Fredrik, thanks for asking." I replied politely, as I lined up my next question.

"Fredrik, may I ask what you know of the old man who sits outside every day on that bench?"

He smiled as he poured, replying.

"Oh, that's just Hans. Nobody knows much about him to be honest, he's harmless enough though. I think he had a family bereavement a few years ago and since then, he doesn't speak. He's usually at the care home but they let him out every now and again."

"Oh, I tried to speak to him the other day, but he just smiled. Didn't say a word."

BY LEE M. COOPER

"Ha ha, yes, he often sits there watching the world go by. I think he used to be a big fan of those American action movies that you have over there. I would say that's probably why he liked you, looking the way you do from out of town I mean," he replied with a smile.

"Do you require anything else sir?"

"No, no that's all thank you Fredrik."

After I finished my breakfast, I walked outside and decided to get a brisk walk into the station, it wasn't far, and the rain seemed to have let up a bit. Unsurprisingly, Hans, as I now knew him, was sat at his usual spot. What the hell, I thought, let's see if I can get anything out of him.

"Hello again, Hans" I said, as I approached him. He sat there with his same vacant smile upon his face.

"Do you happen to know or have seen anything about the mysterious abductions around here?"

Again, nothing... so I tried a slightly different approach. I pulled out my police badge and offered it up to him.

BY LEE M. COOPER

"Hans, I heard you're a fan of American action movies? Well, I'm a police officer, all the way from Chicago. And I need your help to stop the bad guys from getting away."

Amazingly, he turned his head and stared at the badge, it seemed to perk him up a little as he smiled. However, still no words. Instead, he held out his hand, as though he was trying to hold a pen.

"You, you want to write something?" I asked him, searching about my inside coat pocket and passing him my notebook and pencil. He began to write something.

'Kom....deg.......ut'

"Kom deg ut," I read out slowly.

"I'm, I'm sorry Hans I don't understand what this means" I said, quite perturbed. He looked at me briefly, then licked his lips and put the pencil to paper once again. I read it out again, this time in its English translation.

"Get......out."

I didn't know what to think or say to him at this point, what could it mean, if anything? Maybe it was just the

BY LEE M. COOPER

rumblings of an elderly, crazed man. Thinking nothing more of it for now, I decided to thank him for the warning, and move on.

I eventually reached the station, Andersen once again opened the door and let me in. It's strange, I've not actually seen that many police officers walking around the building so far. Maybe two or three, plus the chief. Anyway, after a brief walk-in chat with the chief, he handed me the paperwork he promised me with the addresses on. It was time to get to work.

My first address was not far from the apartment I visited yesterday by the docks. In fact, it was on one of the moored boats there. A miss 'Eva Berg,' and her husband 'Thomas.' As I pulled up just beside the docks around 2pm, all seemed very quiet. The boat, which was a small yacht, looked very normal from the outside, no signs of foul play.

As I went to step on board, I was greeted by another young officer who permitted me entrance, after he said he had been expecting me. However, he did have a serious look on his face, great, what am I going to find this time I wondered. I stepped aboard and straight down into the main living area underneath the main deck. There was a putrid smell, like rotten fish mixed with blood. What the hell was

BY LEE M. COOPER

that?! This time there wasn't any claw marks or gashes around, but as I walked further down the hall towards the front of the boat, I soon found what the chief sent me here for. The smell was coming from a pile of dead fish, literally slumped in the back of the boat. Where the hell did all this come from? No signs of anybody aboard and not even any signs of struggle or disturbance, apart from some photos of the couple dotted around. The creepiest part perhaps, was that all of the heads in the photos were missing...

I stepped outside to get some air and spoke to the officer on patrol duty.

"Hi, I assume forensics have already scoured the area?"

"Yes, officer Hawk, again absolutely nothing came back from them. It's the strangest thing."

Something really doesn't make sense. Are these set ups by someone trying to cover their tracks, maybe throw people off their scent?

BY LEE M. COOPER

Monday February 12th

After a weekend break of walking around town, getting acquainted with the local shop keepers, odd passers-by I met and even the occasional tourist, although they didn't seem to hang around for very long and just passed on through.

And I have come to the conclusion, that this is a cold town. And I don't just mean the weather, the people are strange here...very strange. It's like, nobody wants to help or even acknowledge these disappearances. I've been looking over the notes at the weekend, after the strange wall gashes in the apartment and the unexplained pile of dead fish and decapitated photos on the yacht, I thought I'd try my hand at 52 Sparrow Road for today's delights. This site allegedly, involved a man and his two son's vanishing, with strange writings left behind.

It's 6.30am once again, and after a couple more nights of rubbish sleep, I'm almost getting used to it now. Also, something else odd is happening in my nightmares. I don't see her anymore, I don't see Rachael...all I see is a skeleton,

BY LEE M. COOPER

ghost type creature coming after me. It's dark and I'm running down a narrow alleyway at night. I fall, the creature comes after me from behind and I run & run until I hit a dead end. Then it reaches out to grab me, it opens its mouth and tries to eat me whole. Then I wake up, in a cold sweat...

I downed breakfast with rapid pace, as I was eager to make an early start on today's case. It was actually dry today, just gloomy. The police chief has been good enough to lend me a car from the station in order to further conduct my investigations. I make a short journey to 52 Sparrow Road, it's quite a charming little street, overlooking a hill by the sea.

Upon reaching the door, there were three uniforms waiting outside. There was also a man stood on the doorstep, in a long beige trench coat, he wore glasses, a shirt and tie and held an A4 size notepad folder, close to his chest. He was talking to the police as I arrived, but soon turned his attention to me and introduced himself.

"Ah, hello. You must be officer Hawk?" he said.

"I am, are the clothes that much of a giveaway?" I replied.

BY LEE M. COOPER

"Yes, you can certainly spot an out of towner around here from a mile away. And if that weren't enough, your strong American accent surely would be, heh."

He seemed to try and force the joke, appearing otherwise somewhat socially awkward at first glance.

"I see, well are you able to assist in showing me the crime scene Mr ah..." I stuttered, waiting for a reply.

"Sorry, Mr Hagen, Charles Hagen. I'm a chief inspector in service to this fine little town."

"Oh, I see" I muttered in a low tone.

"Sorry, it's just the chief never mentioned anything about an inspector being present, that's all."

He looked taken back for a slight second, before shaking it off and tightening his tie with a thin smile. He chuckled.

"Ha ha, that's just like the chief. He may not have mentioned me, but I am also working on the case. Anyway, shall we? Two heads are better than one, as they say after all."

BY LEE M. COOPER

The uniformed men stepped aside, and inspector Hagen offered up the way in for me. I nodded to him as I pushed my way through the door into a somewhat generous sized hallway, with stairs just off from it. Immediately I begin to see the strange markings all around, they look to be written in blood but…it's not. There's a strange odour but this time it's as though burning flesh had been present. As I slowly make my way down the hall, I try to decipher the markings, they look as though they were aggressively written, in a panic almost. However, I cannot make out the words or even the language…none of it seems even remotely reminiscent of any language I've ever seen.

"Incredible, isn't it?" Hagen said.

"Well, I guess that's one way of putting it. What language is this?"

"We don't know. It is not any kind of native dialect, nor is it any written language dead or alive that we know of in Earth's history."

That statement bewildered me somewhat. Were these the markings of some sort of madman or some drugged-up kids perhaps, I thought to myself.

BY LEE M. COOPER

"Could it just be someone has left these here to confuse us? Or maybe they had some sort of mental issues, inspector Hagen?"

"Hmmm, possibly. Though the writing style...there's something about the almost...how would you say...etching like style, of it. As though something wild had carved into it. Feel the letters, they have slight grooves in them."

"Jeez...its left behind some coarseness too, similar to what we found the other day in the apartment block, only not as deep."

This was so bizarre; how could any kind of wild beast carve so intricately though? If nothing else, this case certainly had piqued my interest and looked to challenge my skills in the last few days, so far. The writings continued throughout the house, in every room we looked in. Everything else seemed oddly untouched. Nothing else in the whole house in fact, seemed out of place except for the obvious disappearances and the markings.

After an hour or two of surveying the house, I decided to part ways with the chief inspector. He seemed a strange guy, very jerky and socially awkward but also mesmerized

BY LEE M. COOPER

somewhat, by this case. He advised upon our parting, that we may cross paths again on one of the other crime scenes perhaps...I can't wait. Regardless, I now have even more to think about and I'm still none the wiser on any leads thus far. 7pm soon came around, and I'd now begun to make a little spider chart in my room of the findings up to now. Disappearances, rotten fish, decapitated heads in photos, strange illegible markings on the wall...what could it all mean? I decided I needed a mental break and thought a trip down to the bar would do me good.

"Officer Hawk, what ails you sir? The case I assume?" asked Fredrik.

"Yes" I replied in a low, annoyed tone as I swirled my whiskey in the glass.

"Ah I see sir, I see. You know, you are not the first to investigate this case. That is why the cases go unsolved for so long, and they have reached your ears in America."

His poking into my affairs are becoming irritating, so I say nothing and continue to knock back big gulps of my drink, hoping he will take the hint, without me having to be too rude.

BY LEE M. COOPER

"Officer Hawk, as you are an outsider, you may not be accustomed to our ways here, or our history."

"What is that supposed to mean?" I reply.

"Well, a lot of people here in Holberg are superstitious. Many think that these strange goings on and inexplainable occurrences, are down to the monster of Holberg, sir."

'Oh great,' I thought, this is all I need. Now this guy's going to tell me that some monster haunts the town. You know what, I thought, let's see where this goes...I could do with the entertainment.

"Indulge me...please" I reply to him.

"Well sir, the stories tell of many, many years ago when this town was nothing more than a simple fishing village operated by our forefathers. Legend says that the fishermen would often see inexplainable shapes in the water. See strange shadows and hear horrific noises, like some wild beast was stalking them. They would say that if anyone in the village had angered the gods of old, then the great Norse god Odin, would punish them by sending a hell hound of sorts, to eat all the fish and punish the wicked, leaving the rest to starve. And likewise, once the gods felt

BY LEE M. COOPER

they had appeased them and redeemed themselves, Odin would send his son, Thor, to come and drive off the hell hound once more. And thus, this cycle would reoccur again and again."

I stared at Fredrik in sheer amazement, not because I thought he was talking a load of crap or the drink was getting to me, but because I had never heard such an intriguing story.

"Well Fredrik, sorry to sound cynical but, I'm afraid I'm more of a facts & figures kind of guy. If I can't see it and touch it, I don't believe it. But props to that exciting story, I thank you for entertaining me for the evening. Now if you will excuse me, I think I shall have an early night."

He stared at me as though I had thrown him a personal insult for a moment, but then smiled slimly and wished me a good night. Whoever I can pin these crimes on, if it isn't Fredrik, I at least hope I can book him for being a creepy little bastard, at the local station.

BY LEE M. COOPER

Thursday February 15th

I haven't written these past few days, as I've been busy at the various other sites. I've liaised with Chief Larsen and kept him updated with my ongoing investigation. He's a helpful fella, but unfortunately doesn't have the resources to aid me very well. Some more sites I've visited, include a house which is sinking into the very ground. Again, with a missing mother & daughter. And also, a shop which has those strange markings again.

On top of these findings, my nightmares are getting worse still. The strange markings have even made their way in. The past couple of nights, I find myself running down a narrow corridor littered with the red, glowing letters. The corridor grows ever narrower as I run down it, the light at the end drifts further away until the dark beast that chases me, emerges from what little light is left. I turn around to run back, but she's there…Rachael. She cries tears of blood, in a wedding dress and asks me over and over why 'I wasn't there.' God dammit why wasn't I there! It's as though I get trapped between my guilt and whatever tries to punish me.

BY LEE M. COOPER

Good god, it even sounds like this local hell hound is now in my nightmares!

As usual I wake up in a cold sweat, gasping for every breath I take. I'm getting used to the breathing exercises now to get my heart rate back down, funny that it's almost becoming like a routine. Oddly enough as I make my daily rounds of the town, I happen to drive past a little shop not far from the beach, and see constable Andersen stood outside his police car, with a couple of other uniforms. I decided to pull over and see what the trouble was.

"Constable, is everything ok here?" I ask.

"Officer Hawk, no not really. We have had calls about a man with a gun, taking hostages inside this shop around twenty minutes ago."

"What? Please allow me to help" I tell him, pulling out my standard issue Glock 22.

Andersen looked shocked for a moment that I seemed ready to go straight into action I guess, but that's the way I was trained in my advanced rescue tactics course. I don't waste a minute more and make my way over to a small wall next to a skip, for cover. The viewpoint is pretty good

BY LEE M. COOPER

from here, of the glass shop front. It seems small, maybe a grocery store I think to myself. In my training, they teach you how to make every movement optimal, whilst keeping in mind that the enemy may have eyes on you at all times. You can't let them have even the smallest opportunity to strike, and more importantly, you can't afford to allow innocent civilians to get hurt. As I creep a look around the corner, I can't see anyone yet, but I do hear cries and angered shouts. I decide to try and find an inconspicuous entry way, maybe a goods in around the back. Andersen and his men keep their guns focused on the front door, from behind the cars. Good, I'm hoping the criminal inside will be too busy watching them, instead of looking for me. I make my way around to the back as quickly as I can, moving along the low wall to the side and using it for cover. As I keep my pistol up, I slowly and quietly turn the doorknob and fortunately, it opens. The shouts now become more clearer and although I don't understand the native language, it's clear to me that innocent lives are in danger, and I have to move fast. I cannot assume the enemy will take any mercy on these people, and if he sees me, then it's game over for some poor soul. Then I see him, a masked man...maybe some kind of Halloween mask but he has a women held at gunpoint, the cashier I think.

BY LEE M. COOPER

Filling up a bag with the earnings from the till, she's understandably panicked and there appears to be four or five other people in the shop from what I can see. Though, oddly enough it seems as though this is a one-man operation. I'm not sure how he expects to get out, but I don't intend to allow him to get that far, so I stealthily crawl along the back-room floor until I get within five or so feet of the guy. He's big, maybe six foot two if I had to guess, something like that, but my training is all I need. I jump him from behind and wrestle the gun away from him as it lets off a round into the air. The cashier screams before cowering to the floor, as the robber tries to fight back. The element of surprise and momentum is on my side however, and I'm no shrimp myself. I manage to disarm and knockout the guy within a few seconds, and fortunately managed to avoid anything more than a few scared customers today.

Looking down at the mask, I wonder if this could perhaps be our guy. Maybe this is the guy responsible for the kidnappings, or at least maybe he could lead us to others that were. Then again, it does seem strange that someone would go to all the trouble of covering their tracks, only to then pull a stupid store robbery. Maybe I'm clutching at straws, desperate for a lead. Nevertheless, Andersen and his men then come through both the front and rear entrances, as I tell them the problems been taken care of.

BY LEE M. COOPER

"Wow, you American officers really are like in the movies, aren't you!" Andersen jokes with me, as he looks on in amazement and cuffs the guy.

As we get him into the back of his police car, he cusses what I can only guess is a load of Norwegian profanities, then I take off his mask. I don't know what I was expecting, but this guy looked like a plain old, run of the mill crook, not the evil genius I'm hoping for. Damn, I need to start finding some kind of concrete leads, or else my mind will explode.

After the good constable thanks me once more, he drives off leaving me back to my thoughts, as I take a moment to watch the waves crash against the beach below. Deciding the beach may be a good place to clear my mind after the morning's brief excitement, I drive down the road a little ways and park up.

When I was a child, my dad would bring me to the beach, and we'd often kick a ball together or throw a frisbee. My dad was on the force too, and he used to say the beach was his 'escape place.' I now know why. It's a place where the sound of the waves cleanses my thoughts, my guilt. Gives me time to think clearly. Holberg is a beautiful little town in its own, weird kind of way. I lost track of how long I

BY LEE M. COOPER

spent leaned up against my car, just thinking as I watched the waves crash in and out. And then I heard the strangest sound, coming from just off to the end of the beach.

Leaving the car, I decide to run up to the end of the beach, where it meets the cliffs. From what I can see, around the corner, there appears to be a cave...I see flickers of light coming from within. Somebody is in there. I decide to try and free climb my way around, nothing I can't handle. After a short climb, I finally reach the ledge of the cave and pop my head over. There seems to be signs of a small fire in here, the embers dying as though whoever was here had now been gone a while. It still doesn't explain the strange noises I heard, so I lift myself up and shine my torch further into the cave, my pistol raised of course. The cave looks like it reaches back quite a way, but it grows too narrow to fit through. As I hang around for at least ten more minutes, I don't hear so much as a whimper anymore. Was I hearing things? Nevertheless, someone was definitely here...someone is playing games with me, I'm sure of it now.

BY LEE M. COOPER

Wednesday March 6th

It's been around three weeks since my last entry, I've been busy. I have begun to carry out random civilian interviews, in the hope's that I can either gather the intel that I need or catch out the person or persons responsible for these sick games being played. I was hoping that I'd have either solved this case by now or at least be a lot further ahead than I currently am.

I've been making routine spot checks to the cave I mentioned in my previous entry as well, unfortunately I think it's just some homeless person that camps out there sporadically. I've found food wrappers and drinks bottles in there, but still haven't actually caught anyone there...yet. 5.30am and I go to wash my face in the bathroom, looking in the mirror I'm starting to not recognise the face that looks back anymore. My eyes are bloodshot from lack of sleep and stress, I imagine. My beard is coming along...its longer than I've ever had it, just reaching my Adams apple now, if Rachael were here she would probably

BY LEE M. COOPER

have shaved it off for me, heh. The flecks of grey in it, remind me that I'm not getting any younger. I begin to question why I'm even out here anymore. This case, this case is starting to get to me. Since that robber, a few weeks back, nothing of note has come up.

Of the people who I've interviewed so far in the street, fifteen claimed to not know anything about the cases, another twenty-five didn't understand a word I said, and thirty-five more people spoke what I can only imagine were Norwegian expletives to my face before walking off. There's something else that's strange too, I've tried several times now to get in touch with Captain Mulherny on the phone, but every time I try, the call won't connect through. I've even tried driving to the next nearest town and trying from there but...nothing. Theres also no internet in this town, can you imagine in this century a town with no internet? I'm not entirely sure how I'm going to book my flight back at this stage but then again, that's the least of my concerns. I'm not leaving this place until I solve what's happening here.

I visited Chief Larsen this morning, he continues to be a nice guy, but I get the feeling that his patience with my questions and lack of results is starting to wear thin. I think he's convinced that it's down to this 'myth of the town,' regarding this monster that haunts the people. Also,

BY LEE M. COOPER

that Hagen fella keeps appearing from time to time. I find him somewhat irritating. He seems mesmerized by all the evidence but seems to fail to come up with any actual helpful information.

I still see that old man Hans in the town square. He's starting to seem like the most normal person in this town. Though he still doesn't answer me when I speak to him, just the occasional smile. Hey, here's an idea...maybe he's Odin in disguise, from these fairytales and he's watching everyone! Yeah, judging them in case he needs to bring Thor down to beat back this hell hound of theirs. Heh, how stupid. Though that's sounding like my most promising lead right now!

8.30pm, and after another un-fruitful day of findings and still catching no one in that cave, I decide to spend some time in the car watching the sun set over the beach.

I wake up later after having nodded off, wondering how long I'd slept for and looked at my watch. Oddly, it's stopped at 11.30 and the car clock seems to have stopped at the exact same time. Weird. It's pitch-black outside and I decide it's time to get back to the hotel, lord knows what the actual time is. To top off my day the engine won't start, as I try over and over again to turn the engine over. Great, the piece

BY LEE M. COOPER

of shit has conked out I think to myself. So I get out the car and lock it until I can come back in the morning with a breakdown service of some kind. Then I see it. I look over across the sea briefly, and see something white in the distance, it moved towards me with incredible pace and all I could make out was some sort of wavering image. Like…a flag blowing in the breeze. As it approaches, it grows larger and larger as I stand frozen still. Why can't I move? Within the space of a few seconds, a gigantic ship was upon me…if I had to guess, it looked like some sort of old Galleon. Possibly… Spanish? Was I dreaming? It appeared empty as it stopped, it looked worn as though it had seen countless battles. It was painted white; the flags were white too, yet, with a black cross emblem in the middle. Remarkable!

I struggle to think that anyone reading this right now, would believe I haven't lost my mind by now but, it is truly what I saw! No one else seemed to be around, and my body wouldn't let me call for help. I can only describe a feeling, a feeling that compelled me to investigate right there & then. I walked into the water and began to swim out to it; it wasn't far off. It appeared to have stopped only a few metres away from the coastline. I managed to swim up to it and grabbed onto it. This thing WAS real! I could touch it! I scrambled to climb up the side of it, I used cannons that poked through the turret holes as foot grips. That's right, actual cannons!

BY LEE M. COOPER

This is crazy to write, even as I'm writing it I don't believe it! Then, I clamber onto the deck, the deck of this thing! It's deserted as I look around. I'm soaked, and the entire deck looks as though it had been dragged up from the depths. Crumbling and wet through, as I begin to explore the deck I see barrels and old worn rope. Nothing of much interest, at least aside from walking on a mysterious Galleon that is, until I hear a cry. It sounds like a horrible, blood curdling cry coming from below, in what once was I assume, the captain's cabin. I pull out my pistol & torch and proceed slowly down the stairs. As I reach the door, I slowly begin to turn the handle...the cries suddenly stop. What the hell? I wondered what in god's name I was about to find behind the door on this, this ghost ship! To hell with it, I took a deep breath and kicked the door open!

Shining my light around the room, I saw...nothing! There were a few trinkets, a battered globe, and a map on a table. There was also, what appeared to be a captain's desk and chair at the back of the room, with a knife dug into the table. I creeped towards it, feeling myself almost being pulled. And just when I thought this couldn't get any more bizarre, as I reached towards the knife, a body suddenly appeared in front of it, slumped over the table. I can only assume this ghostly apparition, was the former captain of this ship. His hand grasped the weathered looking knife,

BY LEE M. COOPER

looking as though he'd plunged it into the table with his dying breath. As I looked down, it appeared as though it was pinning a letter down onto the table. I pulled the letter out from under the blade, it was written in Spanish, however luckily, I speak a little myself. I translated and read it as follows.

'Get out...it has found us. No, it is too late, the men...those that had not jumped off the ship to their fate below, surely partook in the fate of Odin's pet outside. These being my dying words are thus, the myths & legends are not just that. THEY ARE REAL. IT IS REAL!

It waits for me outside these doors, it cannot cross into this cabin for some reason, and so I would rather starve here than meet the same fate as those poor souls out there.

May God forgive my sins, as I go to meet him soon.'

Signed

Captain Fernando Hernandez.

What on god's green earth, could this mean. Was this a Spanish ship? It seems it must've been marooned somewhere off the coast of Holberg. Was it really attacked by this beast

BY LEE M. COOPER

of legend? I don't know what's happening, but I knew I needed to get off that ship, I thought to myself. I wasted no further time, and about turned to run out the doors. As I did, the deck had changed. It was now filled with rotten corpses, possibly the crew? Blood was everywhere! That scent of dead fish, like on the yacht, had returned. Only now it was very strong. Panicking, I ran to the edge of the boat as fast as I could, to jump...and then I saw the eyes of death upon me. Two glowing red eyes towards the back of the boat, in the shadows. A grumbling, growling sound...I HAD TO JUMP NOW! JUMP BEFORE WHATEVER FOUL BEAST CAUGHT ME! I JUMPED, INTO THE DARKNESS BELOW, THRASHING AND GRABBING FOR THE WAVES, GRABBING AND PULLING......AND...AND...

BY LEE M. COOPER

Monday April 8th

I woke up today, in a hospital bed of all places. I was rather confused as to how I got here, wherever here was. I had tubes in the back of my hand, hooked up to some sort of machine. Beeps hitting on every heartbeat of mine, remind me I'm still alive. A gentle breeze blows a curtain by my window softly. My notepad was beside my bed, and so I knew I had to write down everything that I last remembered.

A nice nurse came to see me around 10am, she said I had passed out and nearly drowned in my car a few weeks ago and had been here in a coma ever since. Apparently a passing coastguard found me and if it hadn't, well I wouldn't be writing this now. She asked me my name; I tell her Christian Hawk. She has a nice voice, speaks English great, just with a slight accent. She seemed surprised that an American would be all the way out here, but explained she understood once she saw my police ID in my wallet.

"A coma?" I ask her confusingly.

BY LEE M. COOPER

"I...I don't understand. Last thing I remember is being on board this...this..." I hesitate.

What do I say next, that I remember being on some ghost ship? They will probably keep me here another month, treat me for concussion or something. Then again, maybe that's what that was. A crazy nightmare brought on by some sort of trauma, after all I did just have a near death experience I guess.

"You American Policeman, you are here to solve these, these mysterious goings on in our town, yes?"

"Well, yes or at least I'm trying to."

"My sister, she knew one of women that vanished. Helga, she was close friend of hers. Please Mr Hawk, when you are better...please find whoever is responsible for these terrible crimes."

Well it wasn't exactly what I was expecting, but the sentiment wasn't lost on me. I nodded with a smile to her, there wasn't much I could do from a hospital bed but so far she seems to have been the most emotionally motivated person I'd encountered here. After she had gone, I pulled back

BY LEE M. COOPER

the bed sheets and with a wobble, I stood with a walking aid that was by my bed. I stumbled over to the window to see if I could tell where I was in this town, as I looked out and finally breathed in the first gasps of fresh air I'd had in weeks, I honestly couldn't determine where abouts I was. There seemed to be plenty of trees, a few benches below with older patients sat on them. However there was no clear view to try and ascertain my position here.

Damn, I'm so confused right now. About everything. How did I get to this place. I must ask and see if I can call my boss, surely someone, somewhere around here has a working line for overseas calls! I decide for now, that I need the rest and clamber back into bed.

I awaken once more after passing out, the clock on the wall said it was 3.43, but it's been that time for at least the past few hours if I remember correctly. Outside looks like sunset, so it must be getting on in the day. I'm not sure if I've had any visitors whilst I was out, but I see a food tray over my bed with what I can only describe as…dog food on a plate. Yuk, I thought but my stomach then reminded me I hadn't had a decent meal in, well I can't remember when if I'm honest.

BY LEE M. COOPER

It had started to get dark outside, and I'd finished what was actually quite a tasty meal. What do I do now, I wondered. I'm bored and lying here isn't helping ease my mind. My mind drifts at times like these, always back to her, back to Rachael. Not a day will ever go by I'm sure, that I won't think about her.

I decide to get back out of bed, my legs could certainly use the exercise. I didn't need my walking aid this time, so I steadily shuffle my way to the door whilst unplugging the cables and wires out of me. A touch of a random button silences the machine from alerting any doctors, as I slowly and quietly begin to open the room's door into the hallway. Peeping out with one eye, tells me the coast looks clear. It's a dimly lit corridor with different rooms like mine, joining off from it. Hmm, let's see what I can see out here I think to myself, and against better judgment, I sneak out of my room. My training comes in handy here to hide away from the odd patrolling nurse, but I just want to get a better viewpoint. I walk towards the end of the corridor and make a left at the junction. Following this hallway down, I see a set of elevator doors at the end and a stairwell. The elevator is too obvious to be caught on, however if I could get a higher vantage point using the stairs…

BY LEE M. COOPER

I walk up a couple of flights of stairs, my legs don't seem to be slowing me down any now, so I start to get cocky. This patient's garment is the only thing holding me back now, I'll never take jeans for granted again, that's for sure. As I arrive at the top of the stairs and push open the doors cautiously, there is only one simple corridor with four or five rooms off from it. I decided to head for the end window, to see if I could catch a better view of where I was. As I approached the window, I could now see the murky lights of the town coming on. It would appear I was a couple of miles out from the town centre, if I had to guess. From here, I could finally make out the top of the hotel I was staying at, also, the docks were just visible in the distance. It seemed this hospital was on the outskirts of the town, but a simple road looked to connect me straight back to the town square.

My mind felt relieved. As a man of caution with slight OCD, I always like to know my surroundings otherwise I feel somewhat uneasy. Being content with my findings, I turned to start my sneaky journey back to my room. The smell in this corridor had begun to start getting stronger, there was always that hospital like smell of chemicals and disinfectant that you usually find, but here…it was quite potent. I walked to the end of the corridor and worked my way back down the stairs, until I hit my next problem.

BY LEE M. COOPER

'Shit! What floor was I on? Well, I remember coming up at least five flights of stairs,' I thought to myself, so let's start there. I worked my way down them, one by one. 'Three...Four...and that should be...Five!' Upon exiting on the fifth floor downwards, I did not recognise this corridor. For one, the colour seemed wrong. I distinctly remembered the walls being a light beige in colour, whereas here, it was more of a pastel blue. Maybe I had gotten off on the wrong floor after all, however as I turned to go back upstairs I heard voices and steps coming downwards. 'Shit,' I thought to myself, I didn't want to get caught. The next best option seemed to be the already open doors to the elevator, so I decided to make a hasty jump in there, and repeatedly pressed the next floor down's button...floor three.

The door slid closed not a moment too soon, as the voices were imminently about to burst through the doors to floor four. As I regained my breath, the elevator started to move, however, it was going back up. What the hell is wrong with this thing, I grunted to myself as I pressed the floor three button with a furious 'bashing.' After it had gone up several floors, it finally seemed to recognise that it needed to go back down to floor three, and so proceeded to descend once more.

BY LEE M. COOPER

'What a piece of shit' I said, hoping somehow that the elevator would hear me.

Then, the next problem arose. A 'ping' sounded, and the weight limit exceeded light came on. I squinted my face in amazement, as the plaque said the limit was 700lbs. Well I knew I couldn't be over the limit, as I only weighed about 170lbs. Was this thing busted or what, I wondered. The other weird thing, was that I felt as though something or somebody, was brushing shoulders with me for a split second. By this point, I was starting to freak out a little, then the light began to flicker. A cold bead of sweat started to trickle down my temple, as I slowly backed myself into one of the corners, glancing around like a madman!
Luckily, after a few seconds the lights stopped strobing, and the elevator began to move once again by itself.

After what seemed like an hour in there, it finally came to a halt, the 'ping' sounded once more, and the doors swung open much to my relief. Darting out of there as quickly as I could, I then turned to survey my new surroundings. Well, this seems like the correct hall at least, pastel blue like in colour. I started to walk towards the end door on the left, my room. What now, I thought as my legs felt like they were turning into jelly. And then the hallway began to blur...I saw...markings, red markings

BY LEE M. COOPER

appear on the walls like the ones I saw before. What the hell was happening? Was the drugs kicking in that they had me on, or was it a lack of? The markings began to bleed as I stammered along, grasping at the walls for support, before I fell to my knees. And then...I saw her. Rachael again, only like in my dreams. She walked out of my room at the end of the hallway, in a wedding dress once again. Only a veil covered her face and the bottom of it was stained in blood. She came towards me, and I screamed back at her.

'GET AWAY FROM ME, GET AWAY FROM ME. YOUR NOT HER! GET AWAY!'

Still, she came at me. Slowly, she paced towards me making horrible gurgling sounds like something from a horror movie! Then, as I fell completely to the floor, paralysed...she took back her veil to reveal a horridly gruesome and grotesque rotten face! It snarled at me once more, worms and locusts ran out from the eye sockets, and I screamed...I screamed like I never had before!

And then...darkness.

BY LEE M. COOPER

Tuesday April 9th

A bright light pierces through my eyelids this morning. At least that is, the sun's rays are beaming through my bedside window, so I can only assume it's morning. I'm not sure if yesterday really happened or was a dream, but it seemed so real.

Surprisingly, I actually feel quite well today for the first time in a long time. The nurse comes in to visit me again. I decide it best not to tell her I've been having delusional nightmares, and she signs a form releasing me. I was a little surprised but whether it was because they needed the bed back for other patients worse off, or that she was eager for me to get back on the trail and find this killer...I could not say.

Just a few short hours later, and I finally found myself at the hospital entrance, leaving this place behind thank God. Another surprise awaited me out front, in the form of Chief Larsen. He was stood outside of a police car, his arms folded with a smile upon his face.

BY LEE M. COOPER

"Ah, at last! It's good to see you out of bed officer Hawk."

His smile grew still, as he walked over to me, and gave me a hand with the small bag I was given.

"Chief, what are you doing here?"

"Oh, I managed to pull a few strings and got you out of there. Wow this is heavy, what are you carrying in here…bricks?" he mused.

"Oh, just some medical provisions the hospital were kind enough to supply me with" I replied.

"Sorry Chief Larsen, what do you mean pulled some strings?"

"Well, I think there may have been a breakthrough in the case whilst you've been away. Come on, get in and I'll fill you in on the way back to the station."

An hour or so later, the chief had just finished his briefing. Apparently, Hagen had been digging into an anonymous tip off from an unknown source. Of course, it would be that smarmy son of a bitch, who finally got a lead.

BY LEE M. COOPER

Anyway, he had basically been fed information about a trafficking gang, operating out of an abandoned factory on the outskirts of town.

"So, what's our next move chief?" I asked him.

"Well, I want you and Hagen to work this case together. You're both the most informed men we have working on this case right now, and I think you will work well together."

'Hmph, we shall see about that,' I muttered in my head.

"Andersen will drop you back off at the hotel, I suggest you get a good night's rest, tomorrow I want you both to head up there and scout out the place. He will pick you up at 0800 sharp."

Andersen had been kind enough to give me a ride back to the hotel. He was still amazed at my actions back with the robbery. I didn't think it was anything particularly special, but the fact he seemed more eager to help wasn't a bad thing. Regardless, I took the short car ride as an opportunity to probe him for his thoughts on the man I'd be working with...Hagen.

BY LEE M. COOPER

"Thanks constable Andersen, for the ride I mean. It's only a short walk back to my hotel...I would've been fine to walk, really."

"Oh nonsense, I won't hear of it. It's the least I can do for your help back with that adolescent robbery incident. Which, by the way, I must say I'm still very impressed with. How you handled it, I mean," he said whilst cheerfully driving down the town's main street, back to the market square.

"Oh really, it was nothing. Back home, in the programme I was in...it was all part of basic training. Hostage situations, disarming the enemy...you know, that kind of thing. Anyway, there's something I wanted to ask you...the chief has put me to work with Hagen tomorrow, to dig into this lead at the abandoned factory? What can you tell me about him? He still seems very...unfamiliar, shall we say, to me."

"Ah yes, he's not around very often...he's kind of called out on a freelance basis. He helps lots of different towns on different cases. I don't think he's been doing it that long really, maybe two or three years now? Apparently, he graduated from Oslo university with flying colours in criminology and psychology. The Chief seems to rate him though."

'Great, smug and a smart ass,' I thought.

"Well, this is your hotel. Is there anything else you need?"

"No thanks, Andersen. You've been a great help. I'll catch up with you at the station, after we stake out this place tomorrow."

Stepping back into the 'Pearl,' the ever-present Fredrik wasn't there for once. Instead, I was greeted by a lovely young lady. She must've been mid-twenties, long dark hair but of a somewhat nervous disposition.

"Hello sir, are you staying with us presently?" she asked with good English, yet a very strong accent.

"I am, thank you. It's Christian, Hawk that is. Is erm, Fredrik not around today?"

The young girl looked at me with a slight frown and blinked a few times as if not understanding what I said.

BY LEE M. COOPER

"Sorry sir, Fredrik?"

"Yes," I replied.

"The helpful gentlemen who's in here most days, I believe he's the manager of this establishment?"

"I, I'm sorry sir. No one by that name has ever worked here. I work shifts here, but the manager is a lady named 'Maria.' She's away at the moment, but if you like, I can leave her a message?"

My face must've shown all the confusion I was feeling at that moment to her. 'Surely, she's probably new and got her wires crossed,' I thought, so I didn't pursue the matter any further.

"No, no that's ok thank you. I must be mistaken, apologies. I think I will just have dinner and rest in my room a little. I've had quite the journey" I said, ending the conversation.

After I had eaten dinner, with a few others in the dining room downstairs, I decided to get an early night for the big day ahead tomorrow. Would we finally get some sort of hard lead on this case, I pondered. Trafficking does sound

BY LEE M. COOPER

like the crime at play here, after all. Though, if that is the case, it still doesn't explain the strange marks we've found. I decide to get some rest, thinking like this all night will only keep me up further.

BY LEE M. COOPER

Wednesday April 10th

You know, Bob Marley once said "You never know how strong you are, until being strong is the only option."

Well right now, I don't feel that strong at all. I can't save Rachael in my dreams, any more than I could in reality. Sleep is becoming a foreign concept to me. Though, I have some sleeping pills in the bag that the hospital gave to me, they helped the most last night. Its 5am, I'm not sure how much sleep I got, but it will have to do.

Today could be a big breakthrough for us, let's hope me & Hagen can co-exist together, long enough to give this town the justice it deserves. 8am soon came around and I was stood on the hotel doorstep, waiting promptly for my new partner to arrive. The sky was murky today, I like to think it's not some kinda bad omen. Looking around, I see the one constant, once more in this town...Hans. In his usual garb, he was sat on his favourite bench, holding what looked like a locket in his hand of some sort. I wasn't about to interrupt his usual meditative state, but this certainly seemed a

BY LEE M. COOPER

different pose for the old man. He seemed to gaze at whatever was in it, without pause.

As I wondered about Hans, Hagen then pulled up in front of me, breaking my concentration.

"Hey! Officer Hawk, hope you have not been waiting too long. Please, hop on in and let us get to work."

Even his chirpy attitude annoys me. Nevertheless, I decided this whole operation today would run a lot smoother if we get along. So I decided to make idle chit chat during the car ride out of town.

"So Hagen…"

"Please, call me Charles."

"Ok, ahem, Charles. Are we the only two venturing to this abandoned factory, no backup?"

"Indeed we are officer Hawk, the chief made it clear that should the factory be, shall we say, less abandoned than it may first appear…then he wants minimal attention" Hagen replied.

BY LEE M. COOPER

"Makes sense, I have my gun...I just hope I don't have to use it. How about you?"

"My Heckler & Koch P30 pistol...never leave home without it. I am surprised you don't carry how you say...erm the big dirty harry gun, like in the movie's ha ha.'

My eyes rolled looking out of the door window, as I turned and gave a brief, forced smile. Where did they dig this guy up from, I wondered. Upon exiting the town within just a few short minutes, our trail took us in a northerly direction. A windy, dirt road of sorts about two miles out of town, culminating in a decrepit looking old factory amongst the hills. From just outside, it offered up a pretty great view over Holberg below. Hagen parked up at a somewhat inconspicuous area just off to the side of the factory. From there it was just a few metres away to the rusted-up entrance. As we snuck around to the side at the front, a steel shutter gate was firmly drawn down and padlocked at the bottom.

Deciding to split up, each of us taking a separate side in hopes of discovering a way in, I took the left side. Drawing my Glock, I once again put my stealthy sneaking skills to good use. The whole building had clearly been vacant for some years, and there was a strange chemical like smell

BY LEE M. COOPER

emanating from within. Where their drugs being made here, as well as kidnapping? Reaching around the back of the building, Hagen had begun to creep up some stairs in hopes of getting through the fire escape at the top, but to no avail it seemed. I signalled to him that I would try the lower left fire exit in front of me. I held my gun in my left hand, aimed accurately at the crack of the door, as I slowly reached my right hand to the rusty door handle...and tried it. To my amazement, it was unlocked! Unfortunately though, it made a rather loud creaking noise, trying to be as quick as I could, I whipped it open as I looked about the dimly lit interior.

Fortunately, this area also seemed derelict as Hagen followed in close behind me. I've been in this job long enough now to know, that any good luck you get...often soon runs out. We stepped in silently and cautiously; Hagen watched the left as I, the right. It appeared mostly dark inside, other than a few flickering dim lights and the occasional hole in the ceiling, which brought some slither of light in. I couldn't say for sure, what this abandoned factory was used to produce, but nothing seemed to work anymore. There were long abandoned conveyor belts rusted to shit, a lot of disused boxes and mainly scrap metal that seemed to be lay around besides that.

BY LEE M. COOPER

"Hagen, you take the left side, I'll take the right" I whispered to him.

At least he seemed to take direction pretty well, I'll give him that. I carried on down the right-hand side of what appeared to be a long disused production line of sorts. There seemed to be a strong smell of what I can only describe as...oil mixed with...blood.

I couldn't see any blood stains anywhere on the floor, as I shone my torch but still, I didn't like it. This place gave me the creeps, and I had a bad feeling about it. I kept my gun held high as I slowly advanced down the narrow side of the conveyor, until I reached the end. There appeared a door, an iron door with a padlock and chains wrapped around it, I wondered what was inside but there was no way I was getting in, not without a set of bolt cutters.

Suddenly a huge bang echoed throughout the tall, wide room as though a set of metal had fallen and hit the ground with a humungous *THUD*! Immediately, this brought my attention and my Glock along with it, to aim over to the left.

"HAGEN! HAGEN!...Charles....?" I whispered sharply across the way from where the noise sounded. However

BY LEE M. COOPER

nothing came back to me...'shit' I thought. I looked around over my shoulder and all around me as paranoia began to set in. Did something happen to Hagen? 'Shit'! What do I do? Was this a set up? Was I being watched? Regardless, my options limited at present, I decided to continue over to the other side of the factory, my paces slow and cautious. Not one more sound echoed after the crash bang I heard, and as I got to the other side, there lay Hagen...looked to have been hit over the head. He was out cold, as I tried to roll him over and wake him, but he was unresponsive. He lay surrounded by what looked to be empty oil drums. What was I going to do now? My backup was down, and someone clearly knew I was here. And then, another sound came back from over the right-hand side. This time, the sound was reminiscent of chains falling to the ground and a creaking, heavy door jolting open.

I had no choice but to leave Hagen propped up against the wall, and hope he'd come around soon enough. Again, keeping my back against the wall, I shuffled back over to where I started.

"Pfftt" I sniggered to myself, as I saw the previously chained up door now unlocked and left open slightly. Someone it would seem, was leading me quite probably, into a trap. But what could I do now, really? I mean if I leave

BY LEE M. COOPER

now and call for backup, my lead that's obviously here would be gone and we would again be none the wiser to solving this case. No, I had to find out who this was, I needed answers dammit! Against my better judgment, I decided to see where our 'friend' was leading me. I slowly pushed open the door, covering the whole of the next room quickly with my flashlight and gun. Checking behind the door also, it appeared as though my lead wasn't in here but must've merely passed on through. This room looked to have had a few rusted-up shelving units with nothing more than dust and debris left on them. The room continued into a narrow corridor with a further door at the end. I didn't like this; I didn't like it one bit. However my mind compelled me to proceed, as though a new addiction had surfaced. An addiction to solving this case and finding out who was responsible. I don't know if it was the town, the time that had passed, the grief I was still processing or a combination of it all that had driven me to madness. But I had to find out...I had to go on!

Slowly, I kept my aim firmly locked on to the far end corridor, as I methodically approached the door. The smell had begun to get worse, though more blood, and less oil was now prevalent in the air. However, not a murmur could be heard in the whole place. I finally reached the door, walking towards it within seconds that almost felt like

BY LEE M. COOPER

hours. Another rusted door, this time however, I kicked it open without further delay and crouched to one knee, whilst still holding my aim high & true. Again, nothing but darkness...and this time some stairs leading down to, yet another rusted up iron door. What the hell was this place used for? Whatever it was being used for now, gave me the creeps. It radiated a sinister energy as I plunged further and further into the belly of this damned place. I crept down the stairs and slowly pushed open another slightly opened door, however this time it led to a further corridor with what appeared to be rooms leading off from it.

The stench here was fouler than anything that had come before it, as I slowly peeked into each room. They were barred, like...cells for something. Was this being used as a prison? They seemed to be basic, a basic toilet in the corner and a hard fold out wooden bench seemed to act as a bed in each cell. However, none of the initial three rooms I walked past, showed any sign of life or that there had been any life in quite some time, it would appear. That all changed as I approached the fourth room, or second on the left...as I shone my torch into the creepy blackened cell, something or rather someone, reflected back at me. I jolted back for an instant, in surprise and horror. I tried the cell door, but it was locked with a padlock.

BY LEE M. COOPER

"Hey! Hey! I don't know if you can hear me, but I'm going to get you out of here. Now, stand back." I said, pointing my Glock towards the lock.

I fired off a round, and it blew the lock open enabling me to access the individual inside. As I leaned down to the seemingly unconscious body and rolled them over, my face lit up in shock.

"Fredrik!? Fredrik, can you hear me?!"

I couldn't believe it; it was Fredrik from the hotel. I searched for a pulse, fortunately I found one. He was out cold, and apart from a black eye and a bloodied forehead...he seemed like he would be ok.

"Come on, let's get you out of here" I said, as I put him into a fireman's carry position, a voice came from behind me.

"Oh, I don't think you will be going anywhere...Mr Hawk."

"What the..." I said out loud, before turning into the butt end of something. And then...darkness.

BY LEE M. COOPER

Thursday April 1st

Jeez...my head. I awoke what I believed was the next day, but I couldn't say for certain. My watch had broken upon my fall. Goddammit, that was a gift from Rachael. Anyway, the only light that came in this cell, was through a small crack in the wall near the ceiling. I don't know who hit me, but I've been out cold for hours. I tried the cell door, but obviously it was locked. Looks like my friend, Fredrik, had been moved. All that was left of him, was a trail of blood, from the floor just below the wooden fold out bed, all the way to the door.

Now I was starting to think I should've grabbed Hagen when I had the chance and run. Hagen...what's happened to him I wondered. He's most probably dead by now, there's no way he wasn't captured, tortured, or killed. Whoever these people are, I'm almost certain now that I'm going to meet the same fate as all those other poor souls. At this point, as I lie here, propped up against a cold brick wall, my mind is drifting to thinking more about the good times with Rachael.

We met when we were teenagers, high school sweethearts I guess you could say. I was fifteen and she was fourteen. We

BY LEE M. COOPER

were in different classes of course, but we studied at the same school. Our friends got to talking one day, after school. We all used to congregate on a park near our homes, we lived at the opposite ends of the same street. Apparently she had a crush on me, and once we got to talking more about what we liked, what our interests were etc, it soon became clear that the feeling was reciprocated. We even both had a shared love of psychology studies, which happened to continue into college together, where we grew even closer. And the rest, I guess as they say, is history.

I can't just sit here. Even if I'm gonna die in this shit hole, I have to at least try, I have to try...for Rachael. She's telling me not to give up. That that's not me, not the kind of person I am. Maybe someone will come check on me before long.

After what seemed like an eternity, with nothing to distract my mind, a bang echoed throughout the corridor, as though a door had opened. It was. Footsteps followed...heavy footsteps. And then as the steps approached closer, a shadow came into view. The silhouette was tall, broad and as the shadow stepped forward his face was covered with a balaclava.

BY LEE M. COOPER

"What! What do you want, you bastard?!" I shouted at the figure.

He said nothing and continued to stare. After an intense stare off, he opened a hatch in the bottom of the cell door and slid through a tray of some sort of food. And then with a grunt, he stormed off and slammed the hallway door shut behind him. A 'cluchunk' sound of him locking the hallway door behind him, reminded me of how hopelessly trapped I was here.

BY LEE M. COOPER

Friday April 12th

After another sleepless night that seemed to never end, I've taken to writing in this journal. I was completely alone, mind you, the odd cockroach that came in and out through the cracks in the wall kept me company most of the night. I can only guess it's around 7am as I write this, a few bleak rays of light are beginning to come in from outside.

I've also taken to playing a new game of sorts with myself, to help pass the time in here. I like to call it...'guess the bloodstain body part origin,' and I'm currently reigning champion at it now. Another thing, this so called 'food' they gave me...it tastes like crap. I mean, bread and water isn't gonna taste great but...it's like it's been seasoned with something. I dread to think what, and after a couple of bites I couldn't stomach anymore. And this bucket they gave me, for a toilet...it need's emptying. Theres only so much I can stomach smelling that all day & night.

A few more hours passed, and my 'friend,' the masked moron, made his unwelcome return. He stared at me again from behind his balaclava on the other side of the cell door.

BY LEE M. COOPER

'COWARD!' I shouted to him.

It seemed to get a rise out of him, since he hastily opened the cell door and marched on in. Maybe antagonizing him wasn't the smartest idea, he packs a hell of a punch, as he knocked one of my teeth loose. The taste of iron filled my mouth, as I spat some blood at him. He didn't like that...he didn't like that one bit. But I knew this was it, this was my moment to get out of here.

He grabbed me by the throat and lifted me off my feet. What the hell was this guy, an Olympic weightlifter or something? He began to choke me with his bare hands, as he made some sort of strange gurgling sound. I managed to kick him in the balls to drop him to his knees, and I followed it up with a few right hooks. Eventually he went down, unconscious. As I stopped a moment to catch my breath, temptation got the better of me. I had to see who this guy was under that mask. I slowly knelt down, feeling my fingers under his chin and carefully peeled the balaclava back.

"What the hell..."

I muttered in disgust, this man, this...whatever it was, almost didn't look human anymore. It was as though

BY LEE M. COOPER

someone had poured acid over his face, as his skin had blistered horrifically, and his teeth looked as though they had been filed down into sharp points. Whatever the hell this thing was, I didn't want to hang around long enough for it to wake back up. I grabbed his keys and ran out the cell without a second thought as I locked it back behind me. Hopefully, that should keep him out of my way until I can find Hagen and get the hell out of here.

As I ran back towards the door I came through at the end of the hallway, it was double chained with two heavy duty padlocks. Whoever ran this place, sure didn't want anyone else coming in and certainly didn't want me getting back out. With my options limited, there was only one way to go. So I ran back down the hallway, pass my cell with the knocked-out freak in it, and tried the only other door at the other end of the hallway. Ideally, I didn't want to go further into the belly of the beast now at this point, but I had no choice.

As I slowly opened the door, it creaked whilst I peeked around the corner. To my astonishment, it appeared to be some sort of lab. There were desks that littered all around the edges of the room, and in the centre lay three huge tubes of some kind. Upon approaching them, the murky water inside revealed what appeared to be some sort of bodies! I couldn't

BY LEE M. COOPER

believe it, they appeared humanoid in shape, but their skin was blistered from head to toe, just like that...that man! The bodies looked like two men and a woman in the centre, if I had to guess since her stature seemed smaller than the others.

'What in god's name is this place?' I muttered to myself in horror.

I looked around and saw a cabinet on the wall, looked like some sort of key cabinet, but upon opening it I hit the jackpot. They'd stashed my gun & badge in here!

'Eureka!'

The brief moment of comfort soon passed in my mind however, as I quickly realised the reality I was in. I walked along the desks, staring at all the computers and papers that were littered about. One flickering monitor caught my attention, it looked to be some sort of email report left on screen. It read as follows.

Day 56, experiment Q-CX1

'The patient seems to be showing signs of consciousness still, and seems resilient to further tests using the Serum X.

BY LEE M. COOPER

This female seems to be more strengthened in both body and mind compared to the other two males. She...or rather 'It' at this point, still seems to acknowledge certain faces and when it is feed time. It seems to react with more aggression, particularly when it sees one of the men who captured it, it would seem. Regardless, we will keep it contained for further studies in the analysis tube.'

I read on in disgust, as there appeared to be further pages in the email.

Day 62, experiment Q-CX1

'The specimen, as we now call it, seems to have succumbed further to the full body blisters that are common with Serum X. Astonishingly, whereas the two male patients seemed to have died shortly after day thirty, this...this specimen seems to only grow stronger and more bloodthirsty! This is amazing! Just yesterday, the specimen managed to break from out of the analysis tube at feeding time, and literally teared apart the handler! It was a beautiful sight to behold. After all our long years of trials, we now finally get to test on real life humans! And not only that, but we are also finally seeing results! Fortunately, the anti-serum darts that we fired at it, seemed to knock the specimen out cold. We must be careful, its blistered skin is

BY LEE M. COOPER

becoming ever tougher, and I fear that these darts won't be able to pierce the skin forever...'

"What the hell, these sickos are experimenting on people here? That's where all the victims have gone. They've become...nothing more than Guinea pigs for this sick cult down here."

I muttered under my breath, as I struggled ever more to read on, yet something compelled me to.

Day 83, experiment Q-CX1

'We are making breakthroughs by the day! For some time now, we have been able to send out the specimen to capture more material for our studies. That's right, it actually is able kidnap victims, as it were. Under the cover of night, however, we have begun to notice a pattern upon its scenes. The specimen is able to grow claws from its right hand, tougher than anything known on earth, from which it secretes a strange red glowing...goo of sorts. We are still examining why this is or how it manifests but I can only assume that it is caused as a side effect of Serum X. The even weirder thing is that it has left strange markings behind at the crime scenes. One can only surmise what this means, if anything!

BY LEE M. COOPER

We hope by day one hundred, that we will have something concrete, in terms of biological weapons, that we can produce to our benefactors.'

Regards

Professor Lovak.

'Lovak.' I pondered. This whole space was empty apart from these, these poor people floating in these tubes. But whatever the case, there must've been some sort of scientists running around here somewhere. And this 'Professor Lovak' finally seemed to be my main lead...along with this 'Serum X' I saw mention of. I'd left my phone at the hotel since I couldn't get any reception anywhere, so annoyingly I couldn't get any photos of the lab. However, I made sure to print out a copy of the emails for safe keeping. With this evidence, I could come back here with a whole platoon of cops and have them swarming the place within a couple of hours. I just needed to now find a way out of here.

I ran to the other side of the room, where another door was situated in this underground hell hole, again I was met with a locked door. So I ran to the other side and tried the door there, at last an unlocked door! Shit! This one was

BY LEE M. COOPER

unlocked but jammed...as though something was propped up behind it. So I tried to put my shoulder into it to 'jimmy' it open. Suddenly I heard a kind of...submersive banging, as though banging a pane of glass under water is the only way I could describe it. The sound definitely didn't come from behind this door...which meant to my horror, as I slowly turned around...one of the test subjects in the tubes looked to have woken up! My heart began to race as I admittedly let out a panicked yelp, and the adrenaline kicked in. Over and over I pounded on the door, trying to shake loose whatever had fallen behind it. However each time, the...the thing behind me started to smack the glass. Harder and harder it seemed to hit the glass, as though it was becoming panic stricken.

My shoulder was starting to give out, but I definitely heard some budging noises behind the door, as though I was loosening whatever had fallen behind it.

"Jesus Christ, come on! Come on!" I shouted, my heart pounding now as though it was about to beat out of my chest!

I turned to look briefly, and the...the thing, looked to have now cracked the glass. It was about to break free! I grabbed my hands around a now sizeable gap between the

BY LEE M. COOPER

door and the frame, as I jerked it back & forth over and over until at last, a bunch of chairs behind it had dislodged and the door now swung open freely! As I was about to run through, I heard the slow cracking sound come from behind me, as though thin ice breaking over water. I looked slowly over my shoulder in complete horror, as the creature inside grew its right hand into monstrous looking claws! Holy shit! I thought, this must've been the same creature from the emails! Without a second delay longer, it swiped upwards and shattered the whole tube that encased it, as grim, black water spewed out across the lab floor. It landed to its feet, making a similar sound to what the guard back in my cell did.

I wasn't about to hang around to be dissected by this monster a second longer, as I turned to run up a flight of stairs. Various brushes, steel pipes and other crap littered the stairs as I pushed it behind me to reach for the door at the top. I finally got there and opened it. Running inside, I shut the door behind me immediately, turned the lock on the door and collapsed some metal racking across it to bar that thing from getting in.

Within this new room, what appeared to be another test room of sorts only this time, there was a desk in the centre with an observation room of sorts in front of it. A foul stench

BY LEE M. COOPER

filled the room, as though a corpse had been left here for about a month. Running towards the other side door, I could now see what was in the observation room behind the glass. It was my old friend Fredrik! Though something felt...off. He was slumped in the corner of the room, with great gashes across his torso. Poor bastard...what did they do to him. Though I was only in that cell, less than 48 hours. He looked and smelt as though his body had been decomposing for around 30-40 days.

WHAT THE HELL WAS GOING ON HERE!

As I was about to leave, I heard a grunting banshee like scream coming from that creature I left behind. It was starting to bash the door aside already. I pulled my gun out and fired a couple of shots off through the door. The thing made a low murmuring groan, and then I heard a thud as though it hit the ground. Still, I wasn't hanging around any longer to find out if it was dead. I had to get out of here and report back to Larsen. I rushed through the door and up another two flights of stairs, in a darkened, grim stairwell and finally out of another door.

The rays of daylight hit my face and what felt like a cleansing. The exit I had found seemed to come out from the other side of the cliff that stood behind the factory. I felt like

BY LEE M. COOPER

shit, and the way back into town would be an arduous one...but I had finally found the horrors of what had been plaguing this town.

I had finally uncovered the truth!

BY LEE M. COOPER

Saturday April 13th

It took me all night and I had now reached into the early hours, but I finally managed to drag my sorry ass back into town. It was pitch black and I'd completely lost track of time by this point, but I'd covered winding roads and barren terrain on the outskirts and to anyone who didn't know me, I must've looked like some sort of hobo.

Upon reaching the door to the police station, I raised my bloodied knuckle to the door and pounded on it with every last bit of energy I could muster.

"Open up! Its officer Hawk, I've found out the truth! Open up!" I persisted.

At last, Andersen opened the door looking somewhat perturbed at my dishevelled appearance.

"Officer Hawk, my god! What the hell happened? We thought you had gone missing?"

BY LEE M. COOPER

"Andersen...please...I need...I need to speak to the Chief. Is he in?"

"Why, why yes he's in his office. You better come on through."

Andersen helped me, as I limped my way down the station corridor to his office and opened the door after a brief knock.

"Sir, excuse the intrusion but..." Andersen started to say.

"Officer Hawk! Your alive? My god, sit down man! Andersen, grab him a blanket and a stiff drink."

"Yes...yes sir!" Andersen said, almost stuttering with panic as he ran out the office to do as the Chief said.

Larsen helped me to a couch in his office and knelt down with a look of concern about him.

"Chief, Hagen...he's...he's. What we found up...what we found up there...it's a place of unspeakable evil. The missing people...the...they...they..." I couldn't spit out my words.

BY LEE M. COOPER

"Christian, please try to calm yourself. Just rest a moment, catch your breath."

Then Andersen came back in, with what looked like a half pint of brandy. I wasn't about to turn it away. As I chugged it back in three or four gulps, I began to compose and gather myself.

"Chief, when me and Hagen left for the abandoned factory we found a way in. Not long after we gained entry, someone or something, hit Hagen on the back of his head. I tried to wake him, but he was out cold. I left him against a wall there, hoping to return shortly after delving deeper into the place. I stumbled across some cells there, which is where I think they were keeping the missing victims. I was apprehended and kept their two nights, before I was able to escape my captors."

Both Larsen & Andersen looked at one another, with a look of great concern as I continued on with my report.

"Things only got worse from there, I'm afraid to say. I stumbled upon what looked like an abandoned lab of sorts whilst trying to find an exit. I came across a report from a 'Professor Lovak' which talked about something called 'Serum X.' Chief, there were three bodies in there. They were

BY LEE M. COOPER

abducting innocent civilians to experiment on up there! I...I know this sounds absurd, but one of the things came alive! Whatever the hell it was, it was highly dangerous!"

At this point, the two looked at me with a look of absurdity. As though I was making the whole thing up!

"Listen, officer Hawk. It hasn't been that long since you came out of hospital with a nasty health scare..."

"IM TELLING YOU, I SAW SOMETHING UP THERE! W... wait...I have a copy of the email...yes, yes it's here in my back pock..."

I searched restlessly, about my clothes. 'Shit!' I exclaimed.

"It...it must've fell out of my pocket as I was escaping. Listen, I know this all sounds crazy, but for all I now Hagen is lay dead up there! Please, send a team up there at least but be careful! Send every man you can chief...every man!"

At that stage I began to drift off on the couch, likely from exhaustion.

BY LEE M. COOPER

"Okay, okay...we will send a search team up there at first light, I promise."

Those were the last words I remember Larsen saying before I passed out.

I awoke a few hours later. The sun seemed to be out, and I couldn't sleep for the horrors even followed me in my dreams. That man, chasing me down dark hallways...leading me right into that thing, that monster! I was in a cold sweat as I woke up on the couch in the Chief's room once again.

"Hey, hey Christian. It's ok, calm yourself. Deep breaths, your safe here." Andersen said, as I came around and gained my bearings once more.

I think he had been left behind to keep an eye on me. I just hope they had taken my mad sounding ramblings seriously.

"Where are the others, did chief Larsen take a squad to investigate?"

"You will be pleased to hear that he took several of the area's best men, armed and prepared in fact. Those were

BY LEE M. COOPER

quite some accusations you were making before. Now you've had a little bit of rest, are you certain of what you saw?"

"Constable, look...one of their brutes knocked a tooth out of mine, as I tried to make my escape out of there. I even found Fredrik dead, from the hotel."

Andersen pulled a strange face as I mentioned this, but then his slight puzzled look drifted on by, as though he was putting down my statement, to shock or something.

I got up and sipped a warm cup of coffee that he gave me, it was actually better than what we had back at the Chicago branch I'll give them that. I walked out of the chief's office with haste, I felt as though I needed to be out there...as though I needed to find out what had happened. I hoped they wouldn't have encountered that, that monster. At least not off guard. Andersen assured me however, that my energy would be better spent here, in the station.

Early afternoon soon rocked around, and my patience was wearing thin. I HAD to know what was keeping them, had they been hurt or worse? What if I'd just sent innocent police officers unwittingly to their deaths. I don't think they were taking what I said too seriously, what if they didn't go prepared after all? All these thoughts were running through my already cracked mind.

Ten minutes later, the chief finally made his return along with several other armed men. To my utter amazement, they seemed totally...well normal.

"Chief! Are you ok, did you find Hagen? Did you find anything?" I said in a panicked outburst.

"Calm down officer Hawk. Well we found the factory alright, but it was empty. We searched every door, every room, every nook & cranny."

"And...well?" I said, hanging onto his response with utter concentration.

"And, well...nothing!"

"Wha...what? What do you mean, nothing? You cannot have searched the area fully. How could you not have found anything?! Give your men to me, I will lead the group back up there myself."

"OFFICER HAWK, SIT DOWN!" Larsen shouted at me, with a blood red face.

BY LEE M. COOPER

"I will not give any more critical police resources, chasing down leads that are not there. Now listen to me and believe me, when I say we made a THOROUGH search of the whole entire area. There was no sign of Hagen, because he called whilst you were asleep and reported that he had gone back home, since you two had been separated on your investigation. He said he was in perfect health and found nothing. Just like we didn't'."

My mind raced backwards and forwards. How could this be? I saw Hagen with my own eyes lay on the floor unconscious, bleeding. I saw Fredrik from the hotel, dead in some gruesome manner!

"Now I suggest to you, that you either go back to the hospital and get checked out for ongoing concussion perhaps or go back to your hotel room and sleep off whatever, 'this,' is."

I looked at the chief and I read the room. They all stared at me with mixed concern and anger, as though I had wasted their time or gone crazy. It was clear that arguing here, now was going to get me no further. I weighed up my options in that moment and decided that going back to the hotel was

BY LEE M. COOPER

my best bet. At least until I could get the chance to get back up there.

"I...I'm sorry chief. Your right, perhaps I'm still feeling the effects of my coma or the med's. I'm sorry, I'll take my leave now and report back tomorrow, chief."

"Make it two days, officer Hawk." The chief barked out as I took my bedraggled, sorry ass out of there.

I walked outside and closed the door, and once again I was in the town of Holberg. Where I had started, and if it were left to the chief, it would appear I was no further forward. Yet, I know what I saw. Some massive brute knocked my tooth out for God's sake. This seemingly extravagant fairytale was not simply something one makes up! I would find the evidence I needed, just as soon as I was rested and could get back up there. I walked on, down the street on a moody day overhead, the few drops of rain almost felt refreshing after the ordeal I had recently been through.

After around five minutes, I came back to the town square. I saw Hans on his bench once more...and you know what, I thought I would tell my 'crazy' story to him, since he seems to be the only one around here who would listen to

BY LEE M. COOPER

me. I approached him and sat down beside him. He was in his usual trance, rubbing the locket in his hand.

"Hello Hans, it's me Christian, the American policeman again. Listen, no one believes me, but I just came back from some abandoned factory on the outskirts of town. I think you tried to warn me about something here when I first arrived, didn't you. I found horrible things up there, in that place...do you know something Hans?"

He stopped stroking the locket in his hand for a moment, as his eyes drifted down towards my hand.

"...Blood...you now know the beast of Holberg" he said in English.

"Hans, you speak English? What do you know? Is this beast a metaphor for this group experimenting on people? Everyone at the station thinks I'm crazy. What do you know?"

He offered over his locket to me, waving his arm as though he wanted me to look at it. I took it from his hand, as he seemed most persistent. It was a pretty, little old thing. Gold plated with a golden chain. He pointed to it again, as though he wanted me to look inside. So I opened it.

BY LEE M. COOPER

"What...this woman...Hans, who is this?"

He smiled, and simply said.

"My light...my wife."

The picture was old, but the strangest thing was, that the picture bore some resemblance to Rachael! A coincidence I was sure of it, and the picture was black & white. Perhaps I was still tired, and my mind wasn't thinking straight. I passed it back to him, and thanked him, closing the locket back into his hand. I decided to go back to the hotel for now, I needed whatever rest I could find right now.
Upon walking into the main reception area of the hotel, I was quickly reminded of Fredrik. The other part of the puzzle which I was still processing in my mind. The last time I was in here, some young girl claimed she never knew of a Fredrik, and the last I saw of him...well he had been gutted to death. Poor bastard. So what would I find on this particular visit I wondered.

What I saw next, made my jaw drop.

"FREDRIK!" I shouted out, my eyes widening in utter shock.

BY LEE M. COOPER

"But I saw you dead?"

He stood before me like a ghost, as though not a day had passed since our last encounter together, when he was still alive. His somewhat disgruntled face, looking understandably confused.

"Sir, I'm sorry sir...if this is a joke, I'm afraid I don't...get 'it'".

I must've looked like a crazed lunatic to him, my eyes tired and bloodshot, covered in blood. Was I seeing a ghost? I had to think of my next move and how to play it carefully. On one hand, I could confront Fredrik and ask what the hell was going on and was he trying to play me for some kind of fool? Or the other option was to play along as though this was some kind of joke and carry on gathering whatever intel I could and find out what was going on in this town once and for all. I decided to go with option b and buy myself some more time. Let's face it, being thrown in a loony bin somewhere wasn't going to help me right now.

"H..ha...haha I got you Fredrik!"

"Oh! Ha....ha ha very good sir! Very good indeed!"

BY LEE M. COOPER

"Ha I'm sorry Fredrik, us yank's have a very different sense of humour to you guys I guess huh? And I must pardon my appearance, as you can see...the case is progressing, shall we say. I've just come to get some rest and a clean change of clothing."

"Ah very good sir, do you require anything bringing to your room at all?"

"No...no thankyou Fredrik."

If that is your name, I thought to myself. The smug son of a bitch smiled at me as though nothing had ever happened. I marched myself upstairs to my room and headed straight for a hot shower.

The fine line between reality and fantasy was becoming ever more blurred to me. I don't know if I have some serious head trauma or if everyone is playing me for a fool here. If I had to take a punt right now, I'd say this whole town is sinister, and there is evil afoot here. The water washes away the blood, but I roll my tongue around in my mouth a little...and my loose tooth finally falls out into my hand. As pissed off as I am about losing a tooth, as I stare at it in my hand...it reminds me that I'm not going completely crazy.

BY LEE M. COOPER

Afterwards I decided to get some sleep, whatever was coming next it could wait until tomorrow now. I locked my door and checked my mobile phone again. Still not one bar of signal, so I throw it back in the drawer. Time for some rest.

BY LEE M. COOPER

Sunday April 14th (AM)

I actually woke up today feeling a lot more refreshed than I had in weeks. I slept right through until around mid-day, but damn did I need it. I opened the curtains and welcomed in a new day in this horror show of a town. Now was the time to carefully plan my next moves, before I get into any more trouble.

No, now my first thought is that I need to somehow get back up to that lab in the factory basement, but next time I'll be prepared. And my Glock alone, won't be enough if I run into that nightmarish creature again up there. No, so my first stop is to find the nearest gun shop around here and get myself properly armed.

I left my room once I was dressed and didn't linger in the hotel lobby. Anymore encounters at present with Fredrik would be uncomfortable to say the least, and I don't much fancy speaking to anyone else unless I absolutely have to for that matter. My safest bet right now, is to assume that

BY LEE M. COOPER

everyone in this wretched town, is in on whatever is going on up there.

I remember on my way into town and a few times since, having passed a local hunting shop. I still had access to the police car I've been borrowing, and so took a ride over there. The place was only around five minutes away, west of the town square. 'Norsk Jaktutstyr' was the name of the shop, simply translated means 'Norwegian hunting gear.'

A I parked up and stepped through the door, a gentle bell chime rung overhead, to announce my entry and I was greeted by a somewhat burly looking man behind the counter. The shop was completely dead inside, and I mean more than just the level of current custom. Taxidermy lined the walls high up, of various deer, birds of prey and other animals with which I was unfamiliar. Below them lay glass counters full of rifles, guns, and all kinds of hunting accessories. As I approached the girthy man behind the counter, he stood straight with a look of distrust at me. He was a tall man, around 6ft 5 if I had to guess and very wide. He had a large grey & brown beard that covered half his face, whilst a store named cap almost covered the other half of his face.

BY LEE M. COOPER

"Hello or Hallo should I say" I chuckled, trying to lighten the room. It didn't work.

"You are American. You police man?"

He seemed well informed of me, though I'm unsure if that were because I'd been around town for long enough now, or that rumours had begun to spread of my possible insanity.

"I, ahm…I see my reputation precedes me. Yes, I am Chicago police officer Christian Hawk. And who might you be?" I asked.

"Hmph!" the man grunted, before relenting his name to me.

"Harald" he said.

"I know your face officer Hawk; chief Larsen has spoken of you before."

"Oh, has he? Hope it is nothing bad haha." I nervously chuckled.

"No! He mentions you in passing, all of his officers come here for their guns, what might you need?"

BY LEE M. COOPER

Phew, that was a small relief. It at least appears as though he doesn't know I came back yesterday, in a frantic panic. If he did, it may have gotten in the way of him potentially offering up his guns to me, if he thought I'd become a madman!

"I am here, because I am close to finding out the culprits of the missing victims in this town. I fear however, that there may be many of them and we need to be well prepared. I am in need of your expertise. The police department and I require your services please Harald."

He looked at me with a long stare for a moment, before suddenly bursting into life, pulling out all sorts of different weapons, this guy had everything short of arming a full military platoon! After a couple of hours, he had given me eight different rifles, seven guns, and had even tried to offer me several explosives! It seemed his quiet demeanour was soon dissolved, once I told him the town police station needed his help. Amazing, it's not always what you know, rather who...

After I had loaded up the car, making it look like Rambo's car, I sat and took a few deep breaths in, and back out again. I stared at myself in the rear-view mirror, and

BY LEE M. COOPER

then up to the hillside on the horizon. This was it, I thought to myself. I'm going to put a stop to this insanity once and for all. And I WILL bring the ones responsible to justice…

As I set off on my rather perilous journey, the sky was murky overhead, but my focus was never more clear. I left the town perimeter just a short distance later and began my trek back up the dusty track towards the factory. Things ran through my mind once more, mainly regarding Rachael. Would I be on my way, to soon be joining her? Maybe if I were, that wouldn't be so bad. I'd either bring this case to a conclusion or die trying.

This had really been the strangest point in my life. I wasn't sure if this was a mid-life crisis or if I was just finally paying for my sins. The town of Holberg was fast becoming smaller and smaller behind me…I wondered if I would be returning there. It didn't take long before I crept up upon the crumbling factory building, but this time, I decided to find the secret exit I came out of last time as opposed to walking into the lion's den, as it were. That 'thing' may be walking around the factory floor for all I know.

BY LEE M. COOPER

I drifted around the back and down the side of another mountain pass, circling some mountainous terrain until I came upon a familiar sight once more.

'This is it, this is the place,' I thought to myself.

I saw the metal door that I'd ran out of mere hours ago. It was closed shut, possibly a retracting mechanism that pulled the door back to, after opening. I parked a few feet away from the door and popped open the trunk. I donned a survival vest that Harald had supplied me with, and attached to it as many shotgun shells and bullets I could. It was made with Kevlar padding. Hopefully, it would be enough to stop not only bullets, but the claw of that damned monster, if push came to shove.

I'd also grabbed a shotgun, rifle and two powerful handguns before closing and locking the car. Having strapped the weapons around my chest & back and bolstering handguns on my belt, I was starting to feel like a one-man army. Anyway, I decided to press on towards the door, I pointed one of the handguns- a magnum, towards the door. If anyone or anything, decided to jump out at me, it was gonna get one hell of a nasty headache once I put a bullet from one of these in its head. I reached my left hand down to the outer door handle, grasping the cold steel...and yanked it

BY LEE M. COOPER

down fast and swung it open, pointing my gun into the dark stairwell.

Luckily, the stairwell was empty...and appeared just as I remember leaving it. 'Oh well' I thought, nothing more to it.

BY LEE M. COOPER

<u>Sunday April 14th (PM)</u>

The last remnants of the fresh air outside, soon dissipated as the door closed shut behind me. As I aimed my gun down the stairs, I also shone my torch for a better view. The stairwell only had two dimly lit, flickering lights and pretty much rendered me blind without it. I tried the door handle behind me, but it seemed tightly locked, as though a mechanism inside may have busted upon closing it.

'Shit! Only one way to go I guess now...' I muttered under my breath.

My heart was beating so hard now, that it almost felt like it was about to burst out of my chest. The steps felt damp and crumbled slightly, as I descended further down towards the door at the bottom. I kept my torch and gun aimed firmly towards it, if anything came at me now I was screwed! This door was slightly ajar from when I'd run through it before, I pushed it open slowly with the end of my gun as it creaked open. This was the interrogation room that I found Fredrik's body in. Amazingly it had disappeared,

BY LEE M. COOPER

just a patch of blood remained on the floor. I looked across to the other side of the room, the shelving units that I collapsed over and a bullet hole in the door from where I shot that thing, still remained. It stank down here; I couldn't tell you what of exactly, but it was a disgusting musty smell mixed with damp in the air. I felt like convulsing just walking around down here. The one thing that made me even more nervous, was just how quiet it was, the only noise coming from a low and dull pulsing sound of power running through the place. The lights flickered in every room down here, I suspected it was down to some sort of damage to the generator that had been caused by the creature, maybe. Either that or some sort of power surge that had blown the power and turned on the backup generators.

My temptation to see if the creature was dead got the better of me, as I immediately had to pace over to where the fallen shelving was. I carefully cleared the clutter away blocking the door, whilst still holding my aim at the already shot up door. Again, I pushed it open, only this time I brought about my shotgun, just in case. As I peered down more stairs, I was amazed...no body, no blood of any kind...

Nothing!

BY LEE M. COOPER

Gazing down the stairs, I knew would lead me back to the lab and where that thing broke out. Or, turning around there was another door to the left of the room I had yet to visit. Again, my curiosity had gotten the better of me and so I decided to try this new door, I needed to see what further answers this may lead me to...or what nightmares.

This door was closed but upon trying the handle, it pushed open with ease. Something about this place seemed strangely unusual, more so than anything else. It was as if someone or something was wanting to lead me deeper & deeper in. Well, they were getting their wish as I pushed open the door to yet another long corridor. This time, it was vividly lit unlike the other hallways and rooms in this hell hole I'd seen so far.

I carefully walked down the long, unsettling corridor, once again smelling a horrid chemical like smell. About halfway down, I came upon a transparent glass viewport into a 'test room' of sorts, I guess you could call it. I could see examining tables tipped over, medical implements of all distinct kinds scattered about and in the centre, lay a giant ominous looking mechanical bed. It had restraints for arms & legs and was covered in blood.

A cold shiver ran down my spine, as I continued to wonder what the hell kinds of experiments they were

BY LEE M. COOPER

facilitating here. As I neared the door at the end, I heard a clattering sound as though something frantically examining a room up ahead.

"Here we go…" I muttered under my breath, lifting my shotgun up.

I was about to find whatever it was I was looking for here. I pushed the door ajar and stepped into yet another lab of sorts. This time I was greeted to a myriad of scientific looking machines, scopes, and computers. Still I heard the rustling up ahead, as though papers and metal trays were frantically being thrown about. I slowly walked down the centre of the room, holding my aim as I saw a glare of light coming from around the far end corner. That was where the source of disruption was emanating from. I began to hear frustrated sounding grunts.

"Eagh……yaarrgghhhhh……where is it……where is it…"

It sounded almost familiar, I swooped around the corner without further delay, and aimed my gun at the back of the mysterious figure.

"FREEZE! DON'T MOVE A MUSCLE. WHO ARE YOU, WHAT ARE YOU DOING HERE?" I shouted.

BY LEE M. COOPER

Before my eyes stood a male, if I had to guess, dressed in a white lab coat, his back turned to me.

"Turn around.... SLOWLY!" I barked at him.

The man spoke before beginning to turn, his words sounding even more familiar to me.

"Officer Hawk...you just couldn't leave well enough alone, could you!"

"Wait a minute, that voice...HAGEN?!"

He slowly turned around, a smug grin on one side of his face. He had on his glasses and a lab coat over his usual civilian clothes. He appeared to be sweating.

"Christian, I have to hand it to you. No one in the last ten years has even come close to discovering what we have been doing down here. You American policemen certainly are persistent."

"I knew there was something off about you Charles, if that even is your real name?"

BY LEE M. COOPER

"Heh heh, no. Charles was the name of my brother, deceased mind you. He was the real genius of the family. You see, around ten years ago, he was the one responsible for creating this top-secret facility. Its purpose, was to research & develop a new serum that could help heal soldiers on the battlefield. He won the Nobel prize you know, for advanced breakthroughs in scientific medicine. Shortly after, he was approached by the government, who were looking to develop a new way to heal wounded soldiers on the battlefield. It was in the hopes of cutting costs funding new soldiers, whilst also pushing this nation's military to the forefront of the world.

Beyond this, it could be used to help the sick, cancer patients...even strengthen the elderly. The most amazing thing, is that after only two years of research and testing, Charles believed he had found the key. The key to unlocking recessive human genes, long left dormant but when activated, can increase the human regenerative capabilities by up to 90%!"

He was visibly getting excited in his mannerisms as he explained this to me, but I wasn't buying it.

"And so those horrible monsters I've seen wandering around here are the result? If so, you can keep your sick little serum. 'Serum X,' was it? I saw the emails lying around here, professor Lovak...you will take me to him, Hagen!"

He smiled even more sinisterly now, the slim, smug grin now covered his entire face, as he gestured with a slight bow.

"Professor Markus Lovak, at your service."
"Why am I not surprised. So what happened to your brother?"

His smug grin turned sour, as though I'd struck a sensitive nerve.

"Charles, he...he died shortly after human tests begun. Five years or so ago now. We were on the verge of a breakthrough, until one of the test subjects went...awry."

"Awry?"

"Yes, a young man who volunteered for the serum. He was a former soldier, crippled from serving his country. At first, the serum began to heal him, miraculously! Within six hours, he was able to stand after having severe nerve damage previously. It was a miracle! Until that is, the side effects kicked in."

BY LEE M. COOPER

"Side effects? You mean the beasts that I've seen roaming around? Those kinds of side effects?!"

"Well, yes in a manner of speaking. You see, what you have to understand, is that to make an omelette, you have to 'break a few eggs,' as they say. And for every 'action' in science, there often soon follows a 'reaction.' The poor boy started to suffer from severe fits and hardened skin. We kept him here for observation but within just twenty-four hours he died. Exhaustion, and his cells had begun to fight against the serum in shall we say, new ways."

He frowned with a look of disappointment, as I continued to quiz the sick bastard further.

"Meaning?"

"Meaning, his heart exploded. But not before swiping at Charles with his mutated hand, as he was trying to give him a sedative. Another side effect you may have seen on your travels around here. It was just the start of a turning point, however. Soon after this, I took over the programme in my brother's memory…and began to perfect what he had started. Now, I have been able to give them

BY LEE M. COOPER

commands...short instructions they are now able to follow! It's amazing!"

I shoved the barrel of the shotgun into his neck, as he whimpered back into the wall.

"AMAZING? AMAZING! Tell me you sicko, what exactly is amazing about turning innocent people into monsters for your own sick experiments? Speaking of which, you say you have been testing on humans for the better part of ten years? So why have reports of missing people, only just coming to light in the last few months?"

"Because, after a few more failures got out, the government pulled our funding. They stopped sending us injured soldiers, ordered us to halt research with immediate effect. So, we had to improvise."

"I see. So you added kidnapping to your impressive resume. And what about the police. Did they not catch onto your little double act?"

"The police? Hahaha" he began to belly laugh. This really got my back up.

"WHATS SO DAMN FUNNY!"

BY LEE M. COOPER

"Well it's just... oh never mind. I'm sure you will find out soon enough."

"What is that supposed to mean? And another thing...Fredrik, from the hotel? I saw him DEAD, HERE! DEAD! And then I see him back at the hotel, as though nothing had happened to him?! Is he something to do with all this?"

Lovak sniggered, looking down at his shoes as he licked his finger and wiped them casually.

"Oh him, yes he's what you might call back home...a 'Junkie.' You see, he is a voluntary patient that has come here time and time again over the years. Miraculously, he's the only test subject in all my years, that I have seen take the serum and not had any side effects. It appears as though his cells regenerate in a way I have never seen before. We are still studying him. He comes back willingly for his 'fix,' from time to time. I suspect what you saw, was the result of him after his run in with subject Q-CX1".

"Wait, so you're telling me that the man just...came back to life? From the dead? His wounds healed, and he

BY LEE M. COOPER

keeps coming back as long as he keeps his lips sealed, right? Is that it?!"

"There is a little more scientific justification to it, but in layman's terms...pretty much, yes."

I was flabbergasted at what I'd just heard in the last ten minutes or so. This town, this place...it was full of demented freaks as far as I was now concerned!

"Listen to me you sick sunavabitch! From what I can tell, the only innocents left here, were the ones that are now dead. I'm turning you in, to the police. Larsen will see you are trialled correctly, for your crimes against humanity!"

I slapped some cuffs on him, he didn't put up any resistance, surprisingly.

"Now tell me, is that...that thing, still out there? Or did I kill it when I put a bullet in it?"

"Heh, officer Hawk. Did you not just listen to a word I said? We experimented on it; to enhance its healing capabilities. So what do you think?" he sneered at me.

BY LEE M. COOPER

"Thought not" I said, before I pistol whipped the piece of shit. Can't deny, that it didn't feel good.

He let out a pathetic whimper, as I grabbed him by the cuffs and pulled him back up to his feet. I spun him around and pushed him forward with one hand on his shoulder, and my shotgun propped over his other, as we began to turn and make an exit out of here.

"What were you searching that desk for anyway, trying to hide evidence were we?"

"Evidence? No. I was just, tying up some loose ends."

I didn't like the sound of that, but it didn't matter. I'd found enough dirt in this place already, to bury this guy a hundred times over and everyone else involved with it! I continued to shove his sorry ass back towards the door I came through, until I suddenly remembered the door I initially came through was now busted.

"Lovak, get us the hell out of here...safely! No funny business, or these walls are gonna get a paint job, understand?"

BY LEE M. COOPER

"Yes...yes...of course, of course. Back down here and up through the stairs is the closest way out" he said.

"No can do. I came through there already, and the doors jammed tight. We will need another way out."

I watched his eyes race around, as though he was looking for a crafty way to trap me. I didn't trust him enough when I thought he was a clean cop, let alone a sinister, human trafficking monster!

"I'm warning you Lovak, don't even THINK, of trying anything on me. If you value your life or your 'research'".

"I wouldn't dare officer Hawk, even I know better than to trifle with a man holding a gun to my face. Follow me, this way. There is another fire escape route we can take through the other side of this lab. It's locked with an 'Alpha' level code, but I have a card key that will get us through."

I didn't trust him, or what he would be leading me to. However my options were limited, and I didn't fancy going back through a dimly lit underground lab with an invulnerable monster on the loose. No I had to persevere for now, no matter how much I disliked it. We soon came to the door he spoke of, and an authorative 'BEEP. ACCESS

BY LEE M. COOPER

DENIED' chimed in with a red light overhead, as we approached it. As promised however, he produced the card key he mentioned, and the door turned a light green. 'ACCESS GRANTED' sounded and the door 'clicked' and slid open before us.

"Move Markus and remember if you try anything funny in here...it will be the last thing you do. Now, where will this take us?" I asked him.

"Do not worry, this is the sample wing where further test subjects were kept. It is empty now however, and the corridor leads to another door. Through that, it is just a short stairwell climb to the other fire escape exit."

I didn't reply and merely prodded him in the back with the gun. He got the message and began walking. The corridor stank of blood and a 'decaying' smell, as though dead bodies had been here for weeks yet the cells we passed were empty, just as he said. The place made me feel sick in my gut, I just had to block it out now as best as I could until we could get out of here. Everything would fit into place then. And I could get the hell out of here.

We made it to the door at the end as he said, and again he used his card key to get us access through. As we passed into the next area, that acted like a break room with a stairwell at the other end, I heard a noise and immediately swung my gun around to my left, to see what it was. I heard footsteps, as a figure emerged from the shadows.

"Good work officer Hawk, you caught the sick piece of crap that we've been looking for, it seems."

"Chief Larsen? What are you doing here?" I asked, visibly shocked, and confused by his presence here.

"I came through the back and down the stairs over there, had one of the boys tail you as I thought you may go off on your own. Looks like I was right! Well done though, I should never have doubted you."

I grinned briefly on one side of my face.

"Chief, thanks. Looks like you saved me the trouble of bringing this creep to you. Do you have a car waiting out back?"

He nodded to me, gesturing the way out for me up the stairs. I shoved Lovak up first, I wasn't taking my eyes off of him for a second. He began to walk up when suddenly from behind me, something hit me in the neck with a severe

BY LEE M. COOPER

blow. I remember falling to the ground and hitting my head on the steps, my vision began to blur. All I could hear was Larsen speak his next words to me.

"Thanks officer Hawk, but I'll take it from here. You see, Markus here is an old friend. We go way back and he's a, shall we say…financial supporter of the Holberg police dept."

I remember him looking down on me, then unlocking Lovaks's cuffs as they both smiled down at me. Those bastards were in cahoots all along! Then all I remember seeing is Lovaks's boot heel…then darkness…

BY LEE M. COOPER

Date Unknown...

I don't have the faintest idea of the day now. I woke with a foggy head, back inside a cell. It was the same cell I'd previously seen Fredrik lay dead in; in fact, I can still see his dried-up blood on the floor next to me. I'd been stripped of my weapons, and there wasn't even a bucket in here to piss in.

Those scumbags did a real number on me, had me fooled from the very beginning. Larsen taking dirty back handers to keep quiet on this place, no doubt probably even supplying him with resources. I looked up through the strengthened glass in front of me, there they were...Lovak & Larsen. Grinning in at me, as though I was some kind of caged animal. They wouldn't have been far wrong; I'd tear them both apart right now if I could.

"Ah, look who's awake? I hope the floor wasn't too uncomfortable for you. Oh and er, don't mind our friend Fredrik's blood down there, if anything it really is miracle-like plasma you know!"

BY LEE M. COOPER

"Shut the hell up you bastard!" I shouted back to Lovak, barely managing to hold myself from jumping at the glass.

"When I get out of here, and I will, I'll kill you myself!"

At this point Larsen stepped in from behind Lovak, his face serious with a touch of almost regret in his eyes.

"Hawk, believe me when I say I didn't want it to have to come down to this. I really didn't. You're a hell of a good officer, your just in the wrong place at the wrong time. A victim of circumstance, if you will."

I gritted my teeth, the chief was no different now to me, than Lovak. He was in on this, and he let it happen. Maybe he's even worse...

"So tell me...chief, what happens now?"

His face suddenly looked deep in thought, as though he was weighing up his options. Lovak on the other hand, wasn't so torn as to what to do with me.

BY LEE M. COOPER

"Let's kill him now, or...wait no! Better yet, I have a new strain of the serum I wish to test. Yes, he will do nicely..."

"NO! He's too dangerous to be left alive, and I respect him enough as an officer, to spare him a fate worse than death. No, I'm sorry officer Hawk. I'm afraid you must die now."

Larsen then began to unlock the door, as he pushed it open he held his gun towards my face and cocked the trigger. There was suddenly a weird noise, coming from above.

"What was that?" Lovak jumpily asked, looking around above him.

"Probably just rats in the vents, I wouldn't worry" replied Larsen.

"Hmph, sound like pretty big rats" Lovak said, in a sarcastically dismissive tone.

"So this is it then, you're going to put a bullet in me and what...carry on? Before you do, I have to ask. Why go to the trouble of putting out a distress call? Why allow me to come all the way from Chicago?"

BY LEE M. COOPER

Larsen blew loudly out of his nostrils, almost sarcastically, as though he found some humour in the question I put to him.

"It wasn't really our intention. However, police protocol states that we had to put out the case to a wider area. I guess you were unfortunately, just a casualty of the situation. Just as I said before. Now, we really must get on I'm afraid Mr Hawk. I have a lot of paperwork to do back at the station."

'Oh well' I thought to myself. Not the way I envisioned myself going out, but at least it was in the line of duty. And I'd see my Rachael again...I can almost see her face right now.

Suddenly the banging from overhead grew louder and louder, as though someone was walking around up there.

"What the hell is that? Is somebody up there?" Larsen said, looking above. He backed out of my cell, locking it again as he climbed a chair nearby and peered into the vent cover with his gun.

BY LEE M. COOPER

To my absolute shock, someone or 'something,' pulled him up! His legs kicked around frantically as he screamed in horror. Lovak ran back out of the door, with a cowardly like scream. The cries from Larsen suddenly stopped and so did his legs, as a pool of dark red blood began to pour down from the vent. His body then fell to the ground, or rather everything but his head!

"Shit, shit, shit, shit…" I said to myself as I retreated into the corner of my cell. I knew what it was…it was that monster. Sure enough, a gurgling cry came from above, followed by its veiny claw bursting through the vent, cutting through it like a piece of paper! It's grotesque body then fell down to the floor…I still couldn't believe this poor soul was once human.

The creature got back to its feet and stared at me for a moment. I could barely make out any human facial features, though a twisted mouth and one eye were still visible, though threads of once long dark hair covered the other half of its face. It staggered over to the cell door, banging into it twice before realising it wouldn't open for it. Still, the thing continued to gaze at me…tilting its head, like a puppy trying to understand.

BY LEE M. COOPER

I pitied the creature, and looking back at it I began to wonder if it would ever find peace. I slowly stood, trying not to make any quick movements. Oddly enough, I didn't feel any immediate hostility from it towards me. I slowly moved to just behind the door, I wondered if trying to commune with it may improve my current standings, such as they were.

"Listen...I...I mean you no harm. I'm just a prisoner here, like you! I cannot begin to imagine what they've done to you or...or even how long you've been here, but I promise you if you can help get me out of here, I WILL stop this happening to anyone else!"

I wasn't sure for a moment if my words had any effect on the creature, or if it even still understood me. However, I remembered Lovak saying he was able to now give the creature basic orders to follow, so it was reasonable to hope it had at least some sort of primitive understanding. It stood and made a low groaning noise for a moment, again tilting its head. Then it reached its claw high up into the air as I darted backwards to the cell wall!

'SSSHHHWWWWAASSSHHHH!'

BY LEE M. COOPER

I opened my eyes after the loud cutting sound and saw it had cleaved the cell door in two right down the centre! However, it didn't seem to want to come inside, instead it stood back, as though to let me pass. My heart raced still, but I had no option but to try and move past it and hope it wouldn't cut me down! I slowly shuffled through the doorway, clambering around the fallen door. I could feel its breath upon me as I moved past it, never taking my eyes off of it for a second. But true enough, it let me pass without harm. The creature stood towering over me, however my presence seemed to calm the beast somewhat, or so it appeared.

"Thank you. So, what now. What will you do? Do you know a way out?" I asked it.

Again, the thing grunted at me, though in a sombre tone. It raised its most human like left arm and pointed towards the way that Lovak escaped through.

"That's the way out, yes? I see... I shall send help; of every kind I can," I said to it.

The creature grumbled once more, almost as if it knew it was beyond help now.

BY LEE M. COOPER

"NN..OOOO......NNN...OOOO...HEE...HHEELLL...HEELLLL PPP...NOO...WWWW" it said, managing to string together a few words still from its damaged vocal cords.

"MM..UU...SSSTTTT.....G..GO........NNO....WWWW"

With that, it made another groan. And then decided to turn away, stumbling back off into the shadows of the lab from whence it came. I didn't understand why it let me go exactly, and I never thought my guardian angel would appear in the form of such a thing. However I wouldn't take this opportunity for granted, and Lovak still needed to be apprehended once more. As I turned to exit the room, I noticed something golden on the ground, shiny. I think it fell from off of the beasts torn rags, that it wondered around in.

I crouched to pick it up, it seemed to be a locket of some sort. Seemed familiar to me, somehow. I opened it up, to find a dated black & white portrait of a young man. There was an engraving, it was worn but there was no mistaking the name upon it, it simply read...

'My love, now & forever. Hans.'

BY LEE M. COOPER

The Day I Escaped...

I still wasn't sure of the exact date, but I decided I'd spent quite long enough here for one lifetime. I ran through the now all too familiar grim corridors, back to where I encountered the treacherous chief before in the breakroom. The door at the top of the stairs towards the back of the room, was swinging open.

"Lovak..." I said between gritted teeth.

Luckily, I found my gun and belongings left on the table at the foot of the stairs, but I only needed my Glock for what I needed to do now. I ran up the stairs after him, and shoulder barged the door open, taking aim all around me as I entered the open outside area, in a furious rage. Looking back now, this wasn't a wise move, I was out in the open and he'd have an open wide shot on me, if he were still around. Though I couldn't help myself, all I saw was red and I made it my personal mission now to bring down this piece of shit for good!

BY LEE M. COOPER

I looked all around me; I couldn't fathom the time, but it appeared to be dusk, and the sun was setting. All I could see was the dusty, mountainous terrain around me. A few high-rise cliffs where he could be...but no, they were too far away and he wouldn't have been able to climb them in so shorter space of time, I thought. The door I exited out from however, was built into a small hill, and so I immediately investigated there first. I clambered up the side of the hill and carefully looked around. There was no sign of Lovak, although I did find footprints set into the sand like ground beneath me. I took the lead, and cautiously followed them over towards the back of the hill.

Just a few feet further down, the hill ended in a short lip overhanging more flat, dusty terrain below. However from here, I seemed to have found Larsen's car and who should be waiting for him there in the driver's seat...Andersen! I carefully and quietly climbed down and dropped to the floor below, sneaking up the driver's side I popped up and stuck the barrel of my gun into his cheek. A surprised Andersen dropped his cigarette onto his pants, in a desperate attempt to put it out.

"Agh! Aghhhh......Hawk...Hawk is that you! Thank God....I...I was so worr..."

BY LEE M. COOPER

"CUT THE BULLSHIT ANDERSEN!" I shouted back in his face through the car door.

"I know exactly what the operation is here. Your beloved crooked 'Chief,' WON'T be joining you anytime soon. Now, where the hell is Lovak?"

"I...err......Lo..Lovak? Hawk, you misunderstand...."

"Save it pal, the next words outta your mouth better be useful ones, or the next thing you'll be smoking is a bullet, understand? Now SPILL!"

His eyes raced around, and panic visibly caught him but before I could get an answer, something jabbed me in the side of the neck, and someone jumped on my back. I fell to the ground as a cold rush ran immediately through my whole body! I struggled to catch my breath and then the cold rush began to turn into an intense burning sensation. I lost the use of my legs, as I reeled on the ground in agony. I looked up, to see Lovak once again having caught the better of me, with some kind of needle in his hand.

"Heh, looks like I got my wish after all huh, officer Hawk."

BY LEE M. COOPER

"WHA.... T....WHAT......DID YOU DO....TO...ME....?!"

"Oh just a little experimental variation on my 'Serum X.' You're the first person to test it, be thankful that your now a part of a possible scientific breakthrough! Ha ha!"

This maniac was going to be the death of me it would seem, but not before I had my revenge. I reached for my gun, which had fallen underneath the car. Andersen got out the car and kicked me in my ribs. Somehow, I don't think my guardian monster was going to save me this time...

"Let's just be done with him, kill him already Markus!" shouted Andersen.

"No! Don't you see, if this serum works then he will regenerate anyway! Though, I'm still not so sure what the side effects will be exactly. It's so exciting isn't it he he."

Andersen bent down to grab me; I mustered all the energy I had left. As he pulled me up, I reached for his gun from his hip, pointed it to his shocked face and pulled the trigger! He dropped lifelessly, as still, the pain rushed through my body as though I was being torn apart from the inside out! I immediately pointed it at Lovak, with a look of shock about him, he tried once more to talk his way out.

BY LEE M. COOPER

"Officer Hawk, wai...wait! You don't want to do this, we can talk things over, turn me in to the authorities...DO THE RIGHT THING FOR GODS SAKE!"

"God has nothing to do with this. This time.... arrghhhh.....this time you die you sick sunavabitch!"

"WAIT! I HAVE THE ANTIDOTE!"

He pulled out a green vial of liquid from his lab coat, as he begged for his life. Regardless, I pointed at his head and put three slugs right in his deranged brain. He fell to the ground...dead at last.

I had no time to breathe a sigh of relief. In fact, I barely had any time to breathe at all. I fell to the ground, slumped against the car. Having no reason to trust Lovaks' final desperate words other than the fact they WERE his 'final desperate words,' I stared at the vial on the floor that lay beside him. Did I take the risk and drink whatever it was?

'What the hell, it can't be worse than whatever I'm turning into here!' I thought to myself.

BY LEE M. COOPER

Out of pure hope that this would put an end to this suffering I was enduring, I picked up the vial, unscrewed the cap and knocked it back in one gulp! Yet again, seconds later and another rush of pain ran through me, though a different kind this time. My vision started to blur, and I crawled through the window of the car, falling onto the rear seats. Slowly, I felt my consciousness begin to leave me.

I wasn't sure if I had awoken into another part of this nightmare, or if I was having a bewildering dream of some kind...but I felt a vivid realism where I found myself. I saw myself, walking through the streets of the town however, everywhere in the shadows I saw red eyes light up in the darkness. It was like I was being watched. I stumbled through the hazy streets, as they began to twist and wave around me, like a heatwave was sucking the life out of this place! I remember looking up and seeing bats flying throughout the night sky, though even they, had a sinister, evil look about them. They each seemed gigantic, with glowing red eyes looking down upon me and screeching a terrible cry.

And then, I remember falling over at the exit to the town. As I glanced up from the ground, I saw a huge flaming portal like whirlwind, sucking up the very town itself! It was as though hell itself was absorbing my surroundings!

BY LEE M. COOPER

'NO...NOOO... NOOOOOOOOOO!!!!! STOP THIS MADNESS!!! ENOUGH!!!!!!!!!!!!!!!!!!!!!!'

BY LEE M. COOPER

Tuesday August 20th

Today would've been our anniversary. If we had married, you and I would've been married fifty years today! Can you believe it...how time flies.

I know I visit your grave most days anyway, first thing every day in fact, but today obviously had more meaning to me than most. Then I come and sit here most days, writing my stories and daydreaming the days away. Imagining what could've been, if only I could've saved you. All I have now, is my pretend world, where I pretend I saved you, and we lived happily ever after.

It's hard though, and it gets harder every day to think of a happy ending. The medication they keep me on, makes my head fuzzy. I still like to imagine however, that I'm the hero of my own story. I do so love those American cops in their action movies, always saving the day...saving the girl. I will keep writing, maybe one day I will find the answer.

The weather today is cloudy again, here in Holberg. No change there, ha! I am an old man now Rachael, but I write

BY LEE M. COOPER

to you still, because you are the only one who truly understood me. The nurses that look after me now are nice and all, but I miss having real friends to talk to. You were always my best friend, and there was never anyone else after you.

My nurses let me out of the retirement home for a few hours each day, but I have to be accompanied as I tend to wander off more & more these days, heh heh. Do you remember that time, that we were invited to your sisters birthday party, and you told me it was fancy dress? I was working late but said I'd catch you there? You played a good one on me that time, I turned up as the only one in fancy dress! Haha I felt so stupid, luckily being dressed as 'Dirty Harry' wasn't so bad compared to my original choice of Buzz Aldrin, complete in a space suit!

Times like that make me smile, though they also make me sad. Even she, your sister, isn't here anymore...nope, I'm the only one left. My dreams get darker and more strange, and I guess that shows in my stories. It's why I cant think of a good ending to save you in them. Must be a side effect of the medication they keep me on.

Well, I have to go now, my nurses have just shouted to me that's its time to get back to the residency for lunch.

BY LEE M. COOPER

Maybe tomorrow I can write a better story, one where 'Chicago cop Christian Hawk' will finally save the day! Heh heh. Until then my love, I will forever continue to keep you in my thoughts.

Yours now and forever,

Hans.

BY LEE M. COOPER

Don't miss out on future releases!

IF YOU HAVE ENJOYED THIS BOOK AND WOULD LIKE TO READ MORE, THEN PLEASE FOLLOW THE ABOVE LINK OR SCAN BELOW, TO STAY UPDATED ON ALL FUTURE RELEASES. THANK YOU.

BY LEE M. COOPER

Printed in Great Britain
by Amazon